MW01122497

This is a work of fiction. Any similarity between the characters and situations within its pages or person, living or dead, is unintentional and coincidental.

All artwork on the cover and within this publication was created beautifully by Haven Cage. The cover model and the photographer are one in the same (Kelson J.)

ISBN 978-1-7771796-01
Published by Kelson J.
Canada

Dedication

To the sweet, quiet, reserved and sexy Russian: thank you for showing me there is light at the end of the sexual tunnel.

To my dear frustrating, mysterious Italian, my forever muse: thank you for always being that proverbial antagonist I knew you would be and for laughing at me even when I couldn't.

To my dear daughters, Amber & Jemma who are both old and young and who will never read this novel: thank you for putting up with your crazy mama's over-sharing and loud phone conversations. I adore both of you and the patience and restraint you both showed me at my time of creative craziness.

To my mom, who will also never be allowed to read this novel even though she swears she will find a way! Thank you for always showing me what hard work and determination look like and for always believing in me even when you may not have agreed with my choices.

Thank you to my baby brothers, Henry & Jamie, who, without emotional and financial support through this process, I may not be here. Thank you for enduring stories about my dating life even when you may have been throwing up in your mouths a little.

Much love to my "team" of kick ass women who helped me put this book together: Kate, Haven and Jenny! All of whom are amazing, talented, gorgeous, strong-minded women who also have a love for the written word and for sharing our realities through our pens!

And finally, to all my "Sophia's," "Veronica's," and "Ter's:" may you forever stand in your truth, find your sexual freedom and never fucking apologize for it!

I love you all!

Kelson J.

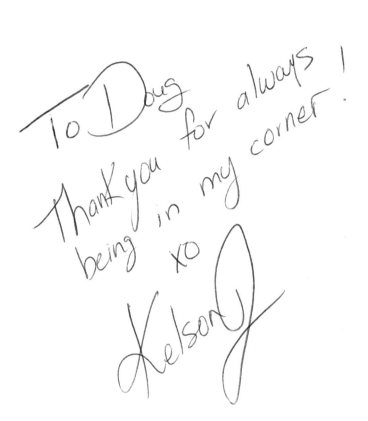

To Doug
Thank you for always!
being in my corner.
xo
Kelson J

A RUSSIAN & AN ITALIAN WALK INTO A BAR…

A Novel

By

Kelson J

PRELUDE

The Bar

"**F**uck, hurry the hell up!" I heard her yell from the front door. "The goddam Uber is here! Ter, you look great, now let's go! And stop checking your fucking phone! He's not going to text you!"

"Shit!" I mumbled under my breath as I closed the screen to my phone and dropped it into my purse. Grabbing my lip gloss off the counter, I quickly threw the finishing touches on to my lips, did one last mirror check and ran down the hall to where Sophia was standing.

"I wasn't checking my phone!" I lied. "I don't care if he texts me! I'm done with his bullshit Sophia!" I couldn't look her in the face. I knew she would see it all over me. I pulled the apartment door closed, glancing in my purse as I did, hoping to see my phone light up as the door slammed behind us.

The bar was packed as usual. And as always,

cover was waived for us as Sophia was friendly with the bouncer. Nodding us in, he glanced at her ass as we walked by. *Typical*, I thought. Sophia just smiled and blew him a kiss as we walked through the doors and headed to our favourite spot at the bar.

I ordered my usual, vodka soda and a splash of cran. Sophia, a beer. The music was loud, and the crowd was already worked up. Lights along the back wall moved in sync with the song playing, candles were lit in the lounge area where most of the VIP bottle service took place. The big dance floor was on the main level of the club near our favourite bar, and it was always packed with people. Mike was tending the bar. He was our favourite server and a guy I had once been crushing on after my difficult breakup. And how could I not? He served topless and his chiseled pecs and abs were more than I could handle. Every time I looked at him, my vagina smiled. He was younger, but I didn't care. He was hot! He had sandy blonde hair, blue eyes and a killer fucking smile. He filled out his tight acid washed jeans nicely, both front and back, and I had decided he was going to be the first guy I fucked since taking single life by the balls – that was, until I found out that I just wasn't his type. And Sophia thought it was funny to tell me.

"You know he likes dick, right?!" she yelled at me from across the table.

"Who?!" I asked.

"Mike! You know, hot Mike who you go

crazy over every time you see him behind the bar!"

My heart was crushed.

"Really?!" I asked. "Are you fucking with me Sophia? He's not fucking gay! He can't be!" I cried as I took a sip of my drink.

She laughed, flipping her hair off to the side. "Ter, I've known him a long time. He likes big ol' cock!" She was laughing louder now.

She saw the look of disappointment on my face as she passed me a shot.

"Don't worry Ter, I will find the right guy for you to fuck! And it has to be soon!" she said. "You're not getting any younger and we don't want that pussy of yours to shrivel and dry up!"

We both laughed.

I knew Sophia meant it and I knew she was on a mission that night. She held up her shot glass, indicating it was time for a toast. I held mine and smiled at her, knowing full well she had something to say.

"Ter, you are too good for that asshole! You no longer are the woman he abused! Stop holding out hope he's going to change. It's time you find someone hot to fuck that will help you get over all the years of crap you've lived through. You are a fucking amazing woman and you deserve to have fun! So, here's to finding fun! Here's to getting laid! And here's to doing whatever the fuck you want!"

I smiled at my friend Sophia, and in that moment, I really wanted to hug her, but I held my shot glass up high and said proudly, "Amen! I will fucking drink to that!"

CHAPTER 1

The Russian

There's something quite sexy and even a little dangerously unnerving about seeing the two men you're fucking walk into the bar you're at, at the same time. I wasn't shocked really. Maybe even a little turned on? I figured at some point it was bound to happen. I mean, you can't get away with screwing two men without them finding out about each other eventually. Right?! I saw them both head towards me at the back of the bar where I stood with Sophia and I thought to myself: I'm either leaving with both of them (if I get my way!), or one of them, but hopefully not neither one of them at all.

I saw the Russian first. That irony didn't escape me since he was the first one I started sleeping with. Oh, the Russian! What can I tell you about him?

His presence was as big as he was tall, standing at six-foot-one from head to toe. He stood there quietly, hovering over a lot of the people around him. His sexiness and alluring grey hazel eyes are what got my attention right from the start. When he looks at me, he makes my heart smile a little, and that doesn't happen often anymore. There's a real shyness, maybe even an innocence about him that first drew me to this attractive Russian. It's his quiet sexiness that makes my panties moist. He's a young soul yearning to take all that this life has to offer him and yet he expects very little in return. That alone made me want to devour him!

Our first date was met with much trepidation and excitement. I was nervous as hell, having just come out of a very emotionally unstable relationship whereby I had most certainly lost myself. I remember almost cancelling on him, twice, even panicking a little that he would cancel on me! But then I thought, what the fuck have I got to lose?! He probably won't like me, nor would I like him; we'd grab a quick cup of coffee, say our pleasantries and call it a good day. Done.

Yeah so that didn't happen.

From the second he walked into the coffee shop, all time stopped for me. I could no longer smell the brewing coffee grinds or hear the loud hum of the room that surrounded me. Everything quieted down when I locked eyes with him as he opened the door to the shop. I thought to myself, *Shit, I'm in trouble now!*

He walked with a perfectly sweet smile on

his face, and as I stood to greet him, he reached out to hug me immediately, kissing me softly on my cheek as if we had already met once before. He smelled so good. And I mean, really good! He smelled like fresh laundry; the kind that comes out of the dryer warm and all you want to do is wrap yourself in it. I held on to him for what I'm sure was only a few seconds, but in my mind that embrace lingered longer than one meeting for the first time would allow.

I liked it. I liked it a lot!

As he looked down at me with those piercing eyes that I could swim in, he asked me in his thick Russian tongue, "Are you ready to go Teresa?" The way he said my name, "Ta Ray Sa," made me want to melt a little more into those damn sexy eyes of his!

Without hesitation, I grabbed my hot cup of coffee and let him lead me to his car.

It was a nice car. Black. Don't ask me to describe the make and model because, well, it doesn't really matter. I did learn however, that his car was his prized possession and one of his first big purchases since moving to Canada. I also learned later that his car was the first place I was going to give my strapping Russian a blow job.

Did I mention how nervous I was on that first date? I think I rambled the entire time he drove to our destination.

As I sat down in his car, my arm brushed against his. I felt this electrical energy race through my veins as I reached toward him to snap my seatbelt shut.

He turned and shyly smiled at me as he asked, "Where should we go, Ta Ray Sa?"

Sigh, I could listen to him speak my name all day long! I thought. And had I answered him with the first thought that entered my mind, I would have replied, to my bed! but I shook away that thought quickly and directed him to drive us to my favourite hiking spot.

As the car approached the parking area, all the warnings my friends had laid on me about the dangers of online dating had escaped my mind. I didn't care at that moment. I felt the Russian was worth the risk. I felt oddly safe with him. I mean, come on, I wanted to jump this man's bones and we had just met! That must have meant something right?

As we headed on foot down the forested trail, I took in all of him I could; his beautiful, kind face, the width of his strong back and square shoulders, the roundness of his ass, and of course the size of his hands. Oh, those hands!

I saw him glancing at me the same way, sizing me up like a lion sizing up their prey before they attack. And I felt this hungry lion just may attack!

He took my hand and smiled down at me as we walked quietly through the woods. The sun was bright, the day was unseasonably hot. It wasn't long before we both felt like we were overdressed, and I didn't think the sun was the only thing to blame for the heat we were feeling that day. I aimlessly pointed out the river's edge we passed along and the fact that the colours on the trees were starting to turn. I tried to make small talk seem bigger when I knew that talk wasn't what the Russian had on his mind. Any chance he got, he would put his arm around my waist, or gently nudge my ass with his big hands while we hiked up a steep hill.

I blushed a little as I heard him say quietly under his breath, "Damn, I love your ass!"

There was that electrical shock once again and I knew this wasn't going to be just a normal date.

As the sweat continued to trickle down our faces and the clothing on our tiring bodies dampened, we looked for a spot to take a rest. I led him through a narrow trail, passing by an old abandoned bridge and down a rocky path to where the river met a creek. We found a spot to sit, looking out at the water's edge that came close at times to our feet. I asked him to tell me about his family from Russia and how he was liking living in Canada. I tried while I spoke not to get lost in his eyes or stare at the softness of his lips. He answered my questions in his nervous accent, drawing me closer toward him with every word. He would smile and cock his head down low and bring his mouth closer to me as he spoke.

His fingers brushed mine and he would gingerly rest them over my thigh where my hand was sitting. As he trailed his fingers up and along mine, I got more and more nervous and more and more excited! I was still trying to play it cool, but I was anxiously waiting for him to kiss me. I hadn't been kissed in a very long time and I wanted his kiss. I wanted to feel his full, soft lips touch mine and I wanted to take in the smell of fresh, warm laundry when he did.

I don't actually remember when he came in for the kiss, but I do remember how he came in for that kiss! He turned to me while I was mid-sentence, nervously giggled at me and went in for the kill. I'm not going to lie, it was kind of awkward at first as it caught me off guard, but it was really nice. But I knew we could do better than nice! His lips, as suspected, felt soft and warm, and the smell of that damn laundry took over my senses as I reached for his tongue with mine. With every circle of his mouth, my body drew closer to his and I felt my breasts resting against his chest. His arms cupped my back and he started to hold on tight. Our breath quickened and my heart began to beat stronger. We got better with each touch of our lips and before I knew it, I could feel his arms leave my back and one hand come to rest upon my heaving breast. The tiny straps of my shirt fell over my shoulder, exposing my lacy bra.

The heat of the sun beat down on us and I felt the sweat from my adrenaline rise. It wasn't long before I felt the tips of his fingers brush along the edge of my lacy bra. Slowly, calculating their way towards my nipple. My heart continued to beat faster, and my body quivered with the excitement. I wanted to feel him cup my breast as he started to kiss the side of my neck. My mind was racing, and I was ignoring the argument I was having with myself about how I really should slow things down. I didn't want us to stop. I was enjoying every minute of his mouth and the feel of his hands touching my body. And that scent! Did I mention his scent?!

The water rushed past our feet, and the hot air continued to make us sweat as we explored each other's bodies with our hands. His chest felt amazing against mine; so strong. As my hand ran up and down his thigh, I could feel the draw towards the bulge in his pants. We kissed feverishly, and I could still feel the nervous energy between us. Stopping occasionally to look at each other, the Russian would giggle under his breath like there was a joke and only he knew the punch line. As I mindlessly guided my right hand towards his crotch, I felt him get more excited. And the bulge below his pants grew. He continued to kiss my neck and glide his tongue down to my shoulder. Before I knew it, it was on my naked breast. My nipple greeted his tongue and my hand cupped his penis that was peeking out over the top of his loosened pants.

There was no stopping us now. *We came this far already, was there a reason to stop?* I wondered.

My body and my mind were having an argument, and all the while my mouth was making its way to his neck. Oh, there was that smell again, and this time it filled my lungs with its warmth. As my tongue ran up and down the Russian's neck, he continued to play with my nipple and cup my breast. Our bodies couldn't get any closer and it seemed impossible that they would even part ways. I didn't care that my ass was sitting on a hard rock or that the sun continued to beat down on us. Nor did I care that we were out in the open where, at any time, someone could walk up on us. I was no longer the woman I was only a few short months before. I didn't care that I had just met the Russian earlier that morning and that I barely knew anything about him. All I cared about in that moment was how good he was making me feel and how it had been a long time since I felt that good!

I don't know how much time had passed as we sat there exploring each other. Time seemed to have stood still. But as we continued to explore, we started to hear voices off in the distance. I don't think this rattled the Russian, maybe he didn't even hear them, but it did bring me out of the trance I was in long enough to put the brakes on and compose myself quickly before our visitors made their way to our sexy sanctuary down by the creek. As we sat still, pretending to look out at the water, we were greeted by another group of hikers who were equally surprised to see us as we were to see them. If it hadn't been such a hot day,

I think the flushed redness of my face may have given away what the Russian and I had been doing not long before they got there. We glanced at each other, giggled a little and got up from our retreat to leave the newcomers to investigate our steamy spot.

He took my hand in his and lead me back up the gravel trail and back towards the forest that gave us some shade as we walked. Neither one of us really talked as we continued to hike through the woods. I was still trying to wrap my brain around what had just happened, and I think he was wondering when we might do it again.

Not a lot of time passed between that first steamy date and the next one. I am pretty sure both the Russian and I were excited to finish what we had started that hot afternoon only a week earlier. He would blow my phone up daily with his little quirky comments about how sexy he thought I was or how he wondered if he might get to experience a "bj" in his car the next time he saw me. I welcomed this kind of playful banter from him. It was never really offensive, as it had almost a youthful tone to it – and not surprisingly since he was thirteen years my junior. I engaged the playful talk and relished the excitement his text messages brought. Daily, he would send me pics from the commercials he was shooting or photos of him and all his sexiness behind the camera. I, in return would send him what I would deem my "sex kitten" selfies showing just enough cleavage to keep him interested. I was new to dating, and online dating was a whole other beast.

It was a Saturday night when I was to see the Russian again. And I knew I needed the perfect dress to turn his head that night. I pulled out my black slinky mini that showed enough cleavage to hug the red lacy bra I wore underneath. The hem of the dress flowed just below the knee and I paired it with a pair of red heels. I loosely curled my hair and allowed the brown waves to sweep across my forehead, teasing them a little with spray. Perfume was sprayed to my wrists and neck, and a subtle, sexy mauve lipstick was applied to my lips, keeping in mind that the Russian had told me that, "makeup was for behind the camera." A few quick glances in the mirror before his car pulled in my laneway and I was ready to go and be devoured by the lion in wait!

Dinner was at a nice, quaint, quiet restaurant. The vibe was cool, as there was art deco on the walls, waitresses with tattoos, piercings and a DJ playing retro music. Multi-colour string lights were draped across the ceiling, giving the space a warm and fun glow. We sat at a small table for two and ordered some drinks; he a beer and me, my usual. I think we were both nervous. He joked, saying, "I'm a terrible Russian, I don't like vodka," and I laughed as I thought he looked yummier to me than the first time I saw him.

He was dressed in a black, tight t-shirt with sleeves that hugged the curve of his biceps and black pants that loosely draped over his long legs. The smell of fresh laundry encased him, and his eyes sparkled when he talked to me. His smooth skin glistened under the lights as the glow cascaded along his freshly shaved jawline and smooth, bald head. With each drink I consumed, I swam deeper into his eyes and with each word that passed his mouth, my eyes didn't leave his luscious lips.

Hanging on every word he spoke, I just kept thinking about how I longed to kiss those lips again.

After several hours of talking and drinking, drinking and laughing, the Russian and I decided it was time to go. He did after all, have a two hour drive to see me and I didn't want to make his drive home a late one. But, standing up from my seat, I felt the warm rush of the booze make its way to my head and a flush feeling overcome my cheeks. I was feeling good and I didn't want our night to end.

As we left the restaurant, he reached over and grabbed my hand to walk me back towards the car that had been parked along a dark side street a few blocks away. His hand felt so good in mine. His fingers cupped mine and as we walked, he twirled his thumb along the inner side of my hand, sending small shivers up my arm. The glow from the alcohol and the chill from the fall evening air allowed me to move my body closer in to his as we walked. Once seated inside the car, with the engine running to warm our space, the

Russian, without speaking, leaned over and kissed me. This time, there was no awkwardness to that kiss, and this time, that kiss had meaning and intention behind it. His lips were so soft, and our mouths danced together like an ice skater gliding along the ice; so smooth and carefree. The windows in the car started to steam up as our engines got hotter. Our hands were racing over each other's bodies as our mouths continued to dance in unison. I could feel my heart beating faster and my breathing getting heavier all the while the Russian still smelling like warm laundry.

It wasn't long before his large hand was cupping my bare breast and the lace of my red bra was now out in the open. Car lights from those passing by would flood the inside of the car but neither of us cared. It was risky, even a tad dangerous and that excitement alongside our horny adrenaline is what kept us going. My hand made its way to the zipper of his pants and it wasn't long before his engorged penis was in my palm. It was smooth and so big as the head peaked its way out from the uncircumcized skin. I gently stroked the shaft as the Russian became more and more excited. His mouth was on my neck, his one hand inside my bra, while the other made its way up the hem of my dress to reach inside my panties. I think he could tell he was making me wet and he got more excited to learn he wasn't wrong.

I don't know what possessed me to do what I did next, maybe it was the alcohol, or the endorphins that were racing through my body or maybe there was just something in the air that night, but before I knew it my mouth was wrapped around the warm head of the Russian's cock. I twirled my tongue around the head and then kissed with my lips down the side of his shaft. The groaning from the car became increasingly louder and I remember hearing him sigh, "Oh, Ta Ray Sa," and I knew that while his hope was for a blow job that night, his reality was much more of a surprise. The more I sucked, the deeper I felt his fingers go into my vagina. It felts so good! I was wet and he was hot! And we were both insane with lust!

Car lights continued to flood past us and the steam from our breaths had now completely closed us in. The engine of the car was running, and the Russian's engine was now in overdrive. The faster I sucked his cock, the louder he got. His hand left my body and was now resting on the top of my head. He gently pushed me closer over his penis as he moved his body up and down in ecstasy. All the while, I continued to tease and taunt him with my mouth. I took pleasure in knowing I was turning him on, and I didn't want it to stop. I was committed now and was willing to take it to the end. But stop it did. He stopped it. The Russian took me by surprise when he lifted my head off his cock and brought my face to his to kiss my mouth once again.

He then paused and looked at me with those grey eyes and said in his sexy tongue, "Where can we go, Ta Ray Sa?"

The heat in the car must have been too much for him to take and I suspected he longed for a place for us to be all alone.

Where could we go? I thought. My mind was racing, and my heart was beating out of my chest. I was too revved up to think. Still flustered and horny, I knew I had to think of something quickly! I didn't want to lose the momentum we had created but I knew I couldn't bring the Russian to my apartment just yet. Sophia was home and I didn't want to let him into my sanctuary where that part of my life was my own.

A hotel? I thought. We could get a hotel room! But I wondered, *Could I spend a night in a room with a man I had just met?* It had been so long since I was intimate with anyone and with that intimacy often brings on a lot of hurt. But I didn't want this moment to pass. I was really enjoying my time with the Russian and I didn't want it to stop.

Finding a hotel late at night and last minute was another story. I think we sat, parked in front of the drugstore where we had gone to pick up condoms, for what seemed like an hour, calling every hotel in town! That nervous energy filled the car.

Surely it couldn't be this difficult for a girl to get laid?! I wondered.

The Russian had pointed out a few of the more seedier hotels we passed on our way to the drugstore asking if maybe we could find a room in one of them. I laughed when I told him they were "seedy," and he didn't know what that meant.

I explained, "Those are where prostitutes or drug addicts hang out."

He laughed saying, "Okay, we shouldn't go there," in his matter of fact Russian tone.

After calling several hotels, I thought we may have better luck if we tried an online booking site. Once on the phone with the woman on the other end, we found an available room within a twenty minute drive.

The woman was so matter of fact when she asked, "So, what brings you to booking a room at this hotel?"

I just couldn't contain my surprise by that question and the nervous energy had built up that I replied, "To have sex!"

Awkward silence on the other end of the phone and laughter in the car between me and the Russian ensued.

As the Russian drove the car to our destination, I kept thinking, I can't believe I'm doing this!

I wasn't changing my mind, but I was certainly second guessing my abilities. It had been so long since I was touched by a man – really touched! I wondered if he would like what he saw under my clothes or if I would remember how to make a man happy in bed? I wondered if it was surely as easy as riding a bike!? Now I was wishing

I had had just one more drink to take the edge off!

We checked in at midnight, with no luggage, to what would soon be deemed our sex hotel. Both of us snickering and giggling under our breath as the man at the front desk slowly took his time to get us set up, both of us wondering if he knew exactly what brought us to his hotel that night?

I felt the Russian put his arm around my waist and pull me close into him as we stood there as patiently as two people could be who were dying to rip each other's clothes off! I remember leaning my face into his shoulder and taking a long deep breath as I smelled the warmth of his skin.

The walk to the room seemed like it took forever and as though we flew there all at the same time. My mind was racing. My heart was beating fast and my hands were shaking. The Russian seemed as cool as a cucumber, but I later learned he's more nervous than he lets on. As the door opened to the room, and the Russian flickered on the light, I slid my one heel off and tossed it against the wall. As I bent over to unbuckle my other shoe, I felt the hands of the hot Russian wrap around my waist from behind me and move me closer to his body.

I laughed nervously, telling him, "Just let me get this one shoe off first."

He laughed, kissing the back of my neck behind my ear. Shivers ran down my spine as I awkwardly tried to get that damn clasp of my shoe undone quickly. Once my foot was free, the Russian spun me around and I was now face to face with him as we slid, him backwards, on to the bed behind us. As I looked into his eyes and kissed his amazingly soft lips, my mind stopped thinking. No longer did I worry

No longer did I worry about how I was going to look naked to him or if I was going to be any good in bed. He took all of my mouth into his and my worries melted away.

This man made me feel sexy, sexier than I had been made to feel before! He was quiet in his pleasure, but he made it well known with his hands and his mouth how much he was enjoying me and enjoying my body. Our clothes couldn't come off fast enough! Articles were tossed all over the room as the passion we felt became more and more intense. How I enjoyed kissing his neck, feeling his strong arms under my hands as I grasped his biceps or felt the weight of his chest on my lips. My mouth made its way down to his cock once again that night and this time I wasn't going to let him stop what I had started earlier. This time he didn't want me to stop!! Feeling him grab my hair with both his hands, made me want to please him even more. Occasionally, I would stop my mouth on the head of his cock, give him a little suck, and then look up to meet his eyes with mine. I enjoyed seeing the pleasure on his face and the big smile on his lips.

Fully naked now and lying on top of the

bed covers, the Russian brought my face with his hands up to his. He kissed me gently. And then he kissed me intensely. The passion between us grew as we explored each other's bodies. A small stream of light shone in through the almost closed curtains. It cast a glow on the two of our naked, sweating bodies as the Russian flipped me over and climbed on top. I was no longer thinking. I was no longer worrying, and I was no longer caring about all the hurt I had just lived through only a half year ago. I heard the packaging of the condom open and a slight pause as the Russian got himself prepared for what was about to come.

As he slipped his hard penis into my vagina, my body tensed up slightly. He gently thrust it further into me as he kissed me on the mouth. His kisses helped me relax and enjoy the feeling of blood pumping through his shaft, my pussy getting wetter with every throb. Slowly at first, the Russian would push his cock deeper into me. And then faster as his and my arousal increased. Faster and faster, deeper and deeper; the moaning I could hear was all mine. I was completely engrossed in the excitement and the freedom I was feeling from having this new man, almost a complete stranger, making love to me. The sweat poured off of us as the bed moved, the sheets dismantled, and the pumping increased.

I heard him tell me, "I'm going to cum Ta Ray Sa," and I got more excited.

I needed to cum with him and I deserved

this. I deserved to feel wanted, sexy, beautiful and desired. And I did feel sexy, beautiful and desired as I felt the wave of ecstasy overcome me, overcome both of us as we climaxed together.

Lying there in the Russian's arms felt nice. I fully expected him to roll over and go to sleep, but instead he held me and tickled my arm with his fingers. We nervously talked about our night and what got us to this point.

I told him, "I hope you don't think I do this often?"

He nervously laughed, saying, "I didn't think so."

I needed to follow up with, "It's not every day I rent a hotel room at midnight with a guy I just met a week ago!"

He kissed me and continued to lie next to me cuddling me as we both fell asleep.

I don't know what time it was when I woke up the first time, but not a lot of time had passed. The stream of light from the curtain continued to cast a glow on our bodies, but our bodies were now cooled down. I felt a chill and knew I needed to get under the blanket somehow, but I didn't want to wake the Russian. Gently, I tried to pull as much of the covers as I could from under my body, covering what I could over myself. As I moved, he started to stir.

He giggled and softly spoke saying, "Here come to me, why are you so far over on that side of the bed?"

He grabbed my body close to his and wrapped both arms around me. The weight of his arms felt heavy and I felt awkward, even a bit uncomfortable knowing he wanted to continue lying so closely with me, but I knew I couldn't fight it. This was a feeling I wasn't used to. He nuzzled his face and mouth into the crook of my neck as I lay on my side with my back against his chest. He held on tighter and I felt the blood flow to his penis making it harder. He rocked his body slowly against mine, continuing to nuzzle into my neck. His hand cupped my bare breast and his fingers began to play with my now erect nipple. My senses awoke and sleep was no longer on my mind as it was no longer on his.

Kissing my neck and my shoulder, he flipped me over and on to his stomach. My hands took each one of his in mine as I raised his arms over his head, pinning them to the bed. I placed my pulsing pussy over his cock and lowered my body down on to his. *Oh God it feels so good!* I thought as I took my time gyrating my hips against his, enjoying every move I made. The Russian was enjoying it too! I opened my eyes and saw the look of complete pleasure on his face and this made me even more excited. It was such a turn on to see the effect I was having on him.

I let go of his hands so they could then be placed on my breasts as I continued to move and sway my body over his. As the intensity grew, he grabbed my ass and held on tight. He helped with his hands to lower and raise me over his cock while I gripped the headboard for support. Fuck! I screamed in my head. This guy was hot, and yay me for getting so lucky to sleep with a man so much younger than me! The mere surprise of a second round was enough to wonder what the morning might bring. We came together once again that night and once again we fell asleep in each other's arms.

Sleep was intermittent. Often, I was caught trying to escape the Russian's hold only to be pulled back into his arms. I wanted to enjoy the feeling of his affection after a long night of screwing, but this was a feeling that was foreign to me. I think he got more sleep than I did as he was the first to wake and jump out of bed. He nervously walked around the room, looking out the window and making small talk about the scene on the street below the window. He checked his phone a few times and went to the washroom, all the while I stayed lying in the middle of the bed, sprawled out on my stomach, naked with only the thin sheet covering my ass.

I tried to pretend I was sleeping but I don't think he fell for it as I heard him say, "Ta Ray Sa, shall we shower and go get something to eat?"

Mmm, the idea of food sounded wonderful, but I was far too tired to move. I motioned with my hand, and mumbled, "Soon, yes but right now I want to keep lying here." I turned my head sideways to see him smile as he then climbed back in the bed, removing the sheet off of me, and placing his hard, warm body against mine. *Could this be happening again?* I thought. This young guy was ready for a third round? I was so tired, but this excited me!

We did eventually make it out of that sex filled hotel room to a place nearby for breakfast; me still in my Saturday night black dress, wet hair from my hasty shower piled a top of my head with an elastic. Small talk seemed imminent since we really didn't know a lot about each other, but the food and our insatiable appetite kept us pretty busy. I had the Russian drop me off at my apartment not long after, to the life he knew very little about. We hugged and kissed each other good-bye and once again I took in that warm, fresh laundry smell, hoping as he pulled away that it wasn't going to be the last time.

CHAPTER 2

My Italian

Sophia grabbed my arm.

"Is that who I think it is?!"she shouted as the Russian walked towards us.

I awkwardly smiled. I saw my Italian was right behind him, but I don't think Sophia had noticed, having only seen pictures of him. Seeing him in the flesh made me weak in the knees! He's so damn sexy! Not as tall as the Russian, but what my Italian lacks in stature he makes up in sex appeal with his thick, dark hair that sweeps to one side across his forehead, and his strong jawline with its dark goatee and mustache. His full lips are as dreamy as his eyes are blue and his body is rock hard for a man his age. The intensity he shows in his face with his devilish grin is enough to make any woman take notice!

The bar was packed, music was loud, and we were standing right by the dance floor. I turned to Sophia and yelled, "We need to dance right fucking now!" as I grabbed her by the wrist and lead her toward the floor, away from the approaching Russian and my Italian in tow.

I knew my Italian would get a kick out of this! He loved the chase. Right from day one he told me so. It was a few months after my steamy first dates with the Russian that I encountered my Italian. The Russian had been ignoring me, or so I felt, so I was back to swiping online. I almost bypassed his profile because, shit, he had no pictures of his face! *Who does that?!* I thought. Only an asshole with a wife hides his face on a dating site! I figured. But not my Italian. Nope. He was not married. Never was. He is not the marrying kind, he said. But he is a mystery! And one I was determined to figure out.

The first time I spoke to my Italian on the phone was a bit of a surprise. It wasn't his sexy, quiet, yet take-charge voice that surprised me but rather what lead up to that phone call. We exchanged some texts over the dating website after we had matched. I was, of course, asking him what his deal was with his mysterious faceless photos, and he had questions about whether or not my pics were recent and how my experience online had been up to that point. I made small talk about some of the dirtier men I had encountered, and he laughed, saying "Well I can see how the guys get looking at your sexy pics. Can't blame them for trying." He followed that up with an immediate, "Just looked at your pics again... Saw some nice cleavage..."

I tried to laugh that surprising comment off with a joke about how he too was sporting some nice cleavage in his faceless, half-opened shirt pic. He laughed saying, "I guess your cleavage was also strategic?"

I don't know what possessed me to keep talking to him really? Something was drawing me to this faceless man who was definitely not shy about expressing where he was wanting things to go, asking me if I "chatted off of here."

I remember typing the digits to my phone number thinking, this is crazy! But also being excited. As I typed those numbers across the chat window, I followed them up by adding, "For when you are ready to reveal yourself," with a wink-face emoji.

He responded in a way that I imagined only an Italian man would. "And will you, too, be ready to reveal yourself?" he questioned.

I laughed saying, "The only pics you will get from this gal are clean pics."

A devil and an angel emoji followed with his reply, "Clean can still be very sexy and the mind can be a dangerous place."

With that, we said goodnight and I waited for him to text me when he was ready. I really hoped he would.

The first time my Italian and I had phone sex was not at all what I was expecting. We had been sending text messages throughout the day with little teases, back and forth banter, taunting each other about our sexual desires. He took command of those text messages whenever he could, but I was no weak opponent. It became obvious to me that he too enjoyed being chased but liked to be the one in the driver's seat; sometimes he would relent, considering letting me take control. I pushed back with replies about how he wasn't the only one with game and that he may find himself evenly matched with me as his fellow Capricorn. That got the goat excited!

The day was long, and I couldn't wait to be done at work so I could spend my evening with my Italian on the phone. He would send me messages throughout the day, asking what I was wearing and demand, "Show me!" As I sent photo after photo to him from the salon, I felt sexier and hotter. He would goad me saying, "You're a tease!" when the pics I sent weren't super revealing. He was making it almost impossible to concentrate on my clients as my mind would trail off to glance at my phone in hopes of receiving another sexy text from him. His responses to my replies pulled me deeper into his world. And I started to wonder if I could send him photos that were more revealing. The idea of fantasy play had never been a reality for me up until now. And I was really enjoying where things were going with this mysterious man.

I couldn't make it home fast enough that first day. Sophia, my roommate and best friend, was already home and lounging in her room. I hadn't told her about my Italian as I was still keeping him a secret. I plopped myself on to my couch, turned on my salt lamp, grabbed a cozy, fuzzy blanket and lay down with my phone in my hand. And I waited, staring at the phone.

And then it happened!

"You home yet?" came across my screen. I got nervous.

"Yes, you?" I asked.

"Yes, and I'm ready to see this game you speak of," he typed. I got more nervous but interested.

I wasn't sure what was to come next, but I didn't let myself think. I followed his lead as he sent text after text asking me to "show him" my bra, my breasts, my panties, my hand down my panties, my face, my lips, and my pink pussy spread open just for him. The Russian and I had never sexted, and so I wasn't really sure how it worked, but I was enjoying my Italian taking the lead. Moments of doubt entered my mind, wondering if he was really who he said he was. Was he going to show my very revealing photos to his friends, or worse plaster them on the internet somewhere? I had wondered. These doubts kept creeping up, but I kept ignoring them. I could feel the intense energy between me and him growing with every picture sent and while it sounded crazy to my rational mind, it was very hot!

So, I sent those photos. And as I did, I investigated his photos with my eyes while my hand was playing with my nipple; my mind trailing to thoughts of how it would feel to have my lips touch his mouth, then his neck, his chest and stomach. My nose would breathe in the warm scent of his cologne as my hands gently slid over every curve of his biceps. I'd let my fingers glide down his chest, resting them at his navel as the wet lips of my mouth made its way to his throbbing penis. I could feel the excitement build with every touch my mind imagined, and as I closed my eyes, I could hear him moan with pleasure.

Our text messages became more rapid. One-word answers followed with each pic we sent back and forth, making it harder to concentrate on the act of texting. The sight of his growing cock in each one made me crave this mysterious man more. I was so turned on, and also a little worried that Sophia would come out of her room at any time. And yet the thought of being caught, also made me hot.

"Call me," suddenly came across my phone and I panicked! He wanted me to call him?

I nervously questioned, "Like on the phone?"

"Call me now!" he typed.

So I did.

When he answered the phone, I think my heart melted a little. He sounded so damn sexy. His voice was quiet, yet in control. With a steaminess in his voice, he asked me, "Tell me how your pussy feels?"

I moaned as I placed my fingers into my now very wet vagina. Hearing him talk to me while I played with myself made me more and more excited. I was no longer worried about Sophia catching me red handed. I was enjoying this new side of me.

As I continued to play with myself, I could hear my Italian on the other end of the phone moaning and asking me, "You like that don't you? You like being my naughty girl!"

His breathing became more rapid and I could hear the flesh of his cock sliding in his hand as he whispered, "You like pleasing me, don't you? You understand?"

I agreed.

"You like being naughty for me, don't you?" he whispered.

I moaned in agreement.

"Tell me you want to please me!" He demanded.

"I want to please you!" I sighed.

"You understand?" he asked once more all the while stroking his hard cock.

"I do," I answered. "I understand!" I panted.

I couldn't believe how horny he was making me over the phone! I had never experienced anything like that before. My past relationships were more traditional, boring really, and this was a new world for me. I was enthralled in the moment and getting more excited with every word he spoke.

As my fingers continued to explore my wet pussy and pulsating clit, I found myself having a hard time containing myself.

With excitement building, I heard myself shouting, "Oh my God! I do! I want to please you!" I cried out as I came into my hand, hearing him cum into his on the other end of the phone.
I lay there for a few moments in silence, just trying to catch my breath and come to terms with what had just happened.

There was an awkward silence; more from my end, I suspect, as my Italian wasn't new to this world of kink play as I was. He chuckled on the other end and broke the silence by asking, "Do you smoke?"

"Smoke?" I laughed. "No, I don't smoke, why do you?" I realized once more that I knew nothing about this man that I just virtually had sex with.

He laughed. "No, but I wish I did right now. It's always sexier to have a cigarette after having sex." We both laughed; that broke the ice and it was nice.

I think we talked until at least one in the morning that first night; he about politics, me about socialism. Nothing in that first conversation was out of the ordinary, and yet, nothing ever got too personal. I could tell he was holding back and being as cautious as I was. I often wonder if his intentions that night were to simply say goodnight and never text me again? But then I must have said something that changed his mind, because during our conversation he got really quiet and then suddenly said to me, "You're a rock star!"

I laughed nervously. "A rock star? Why do you say that?" I questioned.

He replied, "I knew you were beautiful when I saw your pictures, and you're damn sexy, but I didn't know how smart you were!"

It was at that moment that I realized his attraction to me grew not only because of what he could see but because of what he could learn from me. And I think he found me to be a challenge. I thought to myself, *this is going to be good!*

Over the course of the next week, role play with my Italian became dirtier. I mean really dirty! He started teaching me that in play, anything goes. And for my Italian, the kinkier, the better!

My thirst for imagination while sexting with him became strong. I found that with every word I typed, the anticipation of a return text was enhanced. And I knew I could tell him anything because the sexiest part of the play was that it wasn't really happening. We would create different sexy scenarios. I found myself enjoying each and every one of them. We seemed to be able to play off each other's kinks easily and I was discovering a new side to myself. My juices flowed when he would tell me how sexy I was or how hot he felt when he was "talking" to me, his throbbing cock enlarging with every word I typed. And he always liked to show me. Screen shot after screen shot would flood my phone of his hand slowly stroking his shaft. I would take what I could from him as, with each photo he sent, I would have an immense desire to continue to want to please him with my play.

My Italian would express to me how he enjoyed being visually pleased. He loved seeing women in short skirts or dresses, with carefully manicured fingers and toes, and glossy lips. And so I would take care to get dressed every morning with him in mind. The mere thought of picking out the perfect outfit to send him a sultry selfie would excite me. He excites easily over seeing the sexier, naughtier side of me come out to play, and so with every selfie I would send, I would make sure to have my hair done just right or my lips looking wet and shiny. Once I even sent a pic of them with the text, "Imagining your cum on my lips." The dirtier my messages to him became, the easier they got to send.

The intensity with my Italian quickly grew. I was learning that I desired a man who liked to take charge, one that didn't shy away from breaking the rules to "be with me." He needed to be both physically strong but mentally strong as well. During one of our heated "hot dates," as I was nearing climax, I told my Italian that I wanted him to "fuck me with your brain!" And because of this realization, I found myself pulling away from the sexy, quiet Russian, who at times wouldn't text me for days.

This, however, didn't please my Italian when I told him. He wanted to hear about my time with the Russian, explaining to me that, "Hearing about you fucking another man, turns me on!" He got testy with me when I would tell him that I wanted to put my focus towards him. To that, he said, "Then keep me happy, please, be my slut."

Initially the word slut angered me, but my Italian was quick to follow up that text saying, "I will only use that word in play. You know that, right?"

He wanted me to see the Russian again. I told him that I feared the Russian was losing interest in me, having broken one previous date already. My Italian laughed saying, "He will be back when he's horny." He urged me, "Try again, it makes me hot when I know you're with him".

He wanted to know about my time with the Russian, all the dirty details. I didn't fully understand how a man would want to hear about my time with another man. And so, I reluctantly agreed with his desire, making a date with the Russian once again, this time to see a friend sing at a karaoke bar downtown. I promised my Italian that I would send him photos from my steamy date, but wondering if I really could.

I struggled to make that date happen. The less time I was spending with the Russian, the more time I wanted to spend with my Italian, even if was just over the phone. And I wasn't sure where the Russian's head was at. He was often shy with me and not as expressive with his intentions as my Italian. I began to wonder if he was still interested in me. I was missing our time together, but my Italian was keeping me "distracted," as he would say.

I pleased my Italian when I told him that the Russian had agreed to see me again.

He told me, "The thought of you giving the Russian a blow job and fucking him is turning me on!"

He asked if I would be willing to send him a pic of me sucking the Russian's cock. I wasn't sure I believed he was serious in his request and so I told him, "I will think about it."

His less than lack-luster response was, "Fine".

That word seemed sort of final and so I called him on it. I asked him what more I could do for him to take an interest in actually meeting me. "How far do you want me to go to please you?" I asked. "What is it going to take for you to want to meet me?" I pleaded.

His reply caught me off guard but excited me nonetheless.

"When you drive me so fucking crazy that I can't help but want to fuck the shit out of you!" he said. It was in that moment, that I realized I needed to drive my Italian crazy and do what was needed to be done to make him want to keep his promise. I wanted him more than ever!

CHAPTER 3

The Game

While Sophia and I managed to make our way to the dance floor, pushing quickly through the crowd, I could see the Russian making his way to the bar with my Italian right behind him. I wondered if the Russian knew my Italian was on his heels. As the Russian stood with his back to us, I saw him order himself a beer. Justin Timberlake's *I'm bringing Sexy Back* was playing and both Sophia and I were dancing along, trying to not be seen by the two men who I was positive came looking for me. My Italian was just standing at the bar, leaning back on the edge of the bar stool, and staring straight out at the dancefloor. Even though it was packed with people, he had found me and his eyes locked with mine. By the way he was dressed, I just imagined he must smell good, too. He had on one of his typical black button-down shirts (something he had in common with the Russian), and light faded jeans that hugged his small but muscular ass. His shirt was slightly tucked into his pants, exposing the CK buckle at his waist. An expensive watch donned his right wrist and a black leather jacket was flung over his left arm. I smiled slightly at him as I turned away, pushing myself further in to the crowd.

The two men couldn't be any different from one another and yet I found them both hard to resist.

The Russian brought out a sweet quality in me where I longed to kiss his lips and lie in his strong arms for hours. We didn't talk a lot, but I enjoyed rubbing my hand along his bare chest or kissing his lips until mine were raw. His genuine desire to please me was always evident when we were together, and he was always game to go again. My Italian on the other hand, brought out the feisty, anything goes, sex-crazed woman who only wanted to please the man on the other end of the phone. He encouraged me to push myself past my morality and he made me want to be naughty just for him. And by pleasing my Italian, I found myself pleasing the Russian, who then in turn was pleasing me.

My Italian once said to me, "You have the best of both worlds, so why fight it?!" And yet, while this was true, I was still finding myself fighting them both!

The Russian was supposed to pick me up that Tuesday night around seven. I had already confirmed with a few of my friends that we would be meeting them at a local karaoke bar. It's not often I would go out during the week, but the Russian's work schedule didn't always allow for a weekend off and it had been weeks since we saw each other last. I was feeling apprehensive about the date, contemplating seeing the Russian and wishing the date was with my Italian. And so, when the Russian called to say he was going to be bailing on me once again, I got mad. This wasn't the first time he put work before me. And I was beginning to wonder if that was really the truth. Jealousy tends to bring out the worst in me. I don't like to be made to feel as though I'm not important, a feeling that brings up years of trauma and so I usually act out as a result. I'm not proud of this but it's true.

And so, I didn't react well when the Russian disappointed me again, and I told him as much. I think my reaction was also the result of not wanting to disappoint my Italian and the promise I had made to him. I didn't want to let him down by telling him that the Russian had just blown me off. So, I played up the night as though the date was still on. I sent my Italian photos of me getting ready for what he deemed "Your hot Russian date." He wanted to see "what you will be wearing for him, and for me."

I sent him photos of my black, fishnet stockings, my short mini dress that just hugged above the knees, and photos while I was deciding which sexy lingerie to wear for the Russian underneath that cleavage revealing dress. And my Italian ate it up! I teased my hair so that the curls were loose and applied a deep red lipstick that would be sure to pop in every photo I sent.

Once at the bar, I sent my Italian photos from the ladies' room, explaining, "I've snuck away from the Russian, just to send you this pic!" I knew my Italian loved feeling like he was the centre of my attention and I needed to play my cards right in order to keep making him go crazy for me.

He would respond with quick little kiss face emojis having told me earlier in the evening, "I don't want to disturb your time with the hot Russian".

I had such a fun night seeing my friends perform in the karaoke challenge. The drinks were flowing. I didn't want the night to end. It was keeping me distracted from the fact that the Russian had pissed me off earlier that night and the fact that I wasn't sure how I was going to explain to my Italian why I couldn't deliver on the photos I promised him of me and the Russian in bed.

The next morning, I woke up to a barrage of text messages from my Italian asking, "How was your night? Did my little slut have a good time with her Russian?"

"Of course," I replied, praying he wasn't going to ask if I had taken the photos I had promised.

But he did.

"So," he started, "does my sexy slut have any photos to share with me?"

I had to think fast. How was I going to explain what had happened? I feared this would be the end of my sexy Italian and me. "We took pics, but the Russian panicked and deleted them right away," I explained.

"Why would he do that?" my Italian asked.

"His career is important to him," I told him. "I think he doesn't trust me?" I replied.

My Italian was disappointed, but I was sure that would hold him off. After all, he is a career man himself and I figured he could at least appreciate the worry from the Russian.

He asked me when I was going to see him again and I told him "Soon."

Text messages from my Italian seemed to slow down after that. *An entire day went by with barely a word from him. Is he thinking about me?* I wondered. Thoughts about him would race through my mind even when I didn't want them to. I became too distracted at work, barely remembering cutting my client's hair or booking their next appointment. He began to feel like a drug I couldn't kick, and this world of addiction was all too familiar. It's pull would strengthen with every minute and hour that passed without a text from him. I would glance at my phone every time it lit up, having had muted the alerts because they were starting to drive me crazy every time they were not from him. Surely, he's missing me, too? I prayed. He would tell me as much every day, except today. Today was different. I disappointed him last night. I disappointed him because I didn't get what he asked of me. The Russian had let me down and in doing so, I let my Italian down. Today was my punishment. And even so, it made me want him even more.

I began to feel jealous again, wondering if my Italian was busy with another woman? His cold responses to any messages I sent confirmed my suspicions that I was indeed being taught a lesson. I couldn't resist, I needed to find out.

"Are you missing me?" I typed.

"Perhaps," he would reply.

"Perhaps?" I questioned, feeling rather annoyed.

"You broke your promise to me," he stated.

"I told you, he deleted the pictures! I didn't break my promise!" I lied.

"But you didn't send me pics?!" he demanded.

He made me feel crazy! How could I possibly still crave his attention when he was deliberately pushing me away? His replies infuriated me, making my blood boil and my crotch wet!

Why is it that a man so arrogant, so aloof and often condescending, could still be so damn sexy to me?! I wondered.

He made me want to beg for his time and beg for his attention. When he would allow me small glimpses of who he was, I would want him more. And with every text message, good or bad, all I could think about was when we would be together for the first time. I just wanted to fuck his brains out and yet I wasn't sure if he would actually let me.

And so, I gave the Russian another chance. And this time, I didn't tell my Italian.

My town was hosting an annual Festival and I knew the Russian would get a kick out of it. He so enjoyed trying new things and I enjoyed the energy he brought to every date we had. I bought our tickets early and told him to pick me up around three so we could head to our hotel, check in, and cab over to the fest hall. I wasn't ready yet to let him sleep at my place. I felt more apprehension about this date, and also more excited as it drew nearer. I missed the Russian. I wondered if he had missed me. I missed having human contact with a man. My Italian, while sexy, was not giving me any indication as to when we would meet. And I longed to take in the warm, laundry smell the Russian provided me.

He arrived late due to traffic, and yet that didn't seem to matter as time once again stood still when our eyes met. He was so gorgeous! He was dressed in dark ripped jeans that hugged the length of his long legs, a long sleeved dark grey shirt, and a black toque over his freshly shaven head. His eyes twinkled when he smiled at me. He reached over from his seat in the car to kiss my cheek, and all my apprehensions melted away. There was that smell once again and all I wanted to do was to wrap myself in it.

While checking in to the hotel, I felt a schoolgirl giddiness come over me. The hotel was a tad more on the fancier side then what we had previously enjoyed, with a large crystal chandelier in the foyer, dark stained wood trim and an inviting lounge near the entrance. How I loved a beautiful room to fuck in! No distractions of normal life and no fear of having to let the Russian peak inside that part of my life I didn't want to share with him. If time had permitted, I felt the Russian and I would have gotten right down to it, but we knew we had a cab coming and so all we had time for was the dropping of our bags and a quick kiss in the elevator ride to the room. We were alone on the ride up, and the elevator was surrounded by mirrors. When the Russian kissed me, I opened my eyes to see if we looked as hot as I felt we did. I liked what I saw in the mirrors and wondered if this was my Italian's influence on me.

Drinks at the fest hall flowed. We started with a pitcher of beer, but soon graduated to shots. The music was full of energy and the room was filled to capacity. Every time I would leave our table to either go to the washroom or head to the shooter bar, the Russian would follow me with his eyes. It felt good knowing he only had eyes for me and I was glad that I took the time I needed to dress super sexy just for him with my low cleavage showing blouse, my tousled messy hair, dark lined eyes, black, tight leather pants and bright fuchsia lips. I felt good. I felt sexy and thought this was going to be a night the Russian wouldn't forget. And so, I drank some more. I drank to forget my Italian and the promise I had made him. This night was all about the Russian, the sexy, tall, quiet man that took the time to come see me. He deserved this night. And I deserved it with him.

CHAPTER 4

The Twist Tie

T he cab ride to the hotel was quick, or so it felt. The Russian and I had decided around midnight that it was time we head back. I had already broken the heel of my shoe by stumbling through the crowd of people at the festival. I tried to hold on to the Russian's hand and follow his tall, sexiness out the door. He stopped along the way several times to wrap his arms around my waist and pull me close to give me a kiss. The smell of alcohol was coming off the both of us but not in a way that either of us seemed to be offended. The hotel room was calling us, and I could feel that the Russian was just as excited for us to get there as I was.

I sat in the front seat of the car while the Russian took the back. I turned to talk to him while on the drive to the hotel as he held my hand from the back seat, rubbing the top of my hand with his thumb. He would smile at me when he talked, still rubbing my hand. No longer was I thinking about my Italian. I was only thinking about ripping this sexy man's clothes off as soon as we got to the hotel – maybe even in the elevator ride up, I pondered.

As the cab pulled into the driveway of the hotel, the Russian commented, "I need to have a cigarette before we go in Ta Ray Sa." I wish he didn't smoke, but even when he does, there is still something so sexy about him.

It was a chilly evening and I wasn't dressed for standing out doors; broken shoe, a thin revealing blouse, and no jacket. The Russian suggested we go sit in his car that was parked in the lot. While he warmed the car up, the Russian warmed me up by hugging me and rubbing his hands over my arms to create heat. We sat there while he smoked his cigarette and music played on the radio. We didn't talk much. The Russian and I don't do a lot of talking. I fondly remembered how it was not long ago in the same car we had sat in when I first gave the Russian a blow job. I wondered if I might do it again that night, but first suggested we smoked a joint I had rolled and had stashed in my purse pocket as a surprise.

The Russian was game. It had been a long time since I had smoked pot, but I was open to the possibility of trying something new this night. Sophia had given it to me to help with the nervousness I was feeling earlier on about the date. He lit the joint and took a few hauls off it. He laid back in the seat and smiled.

"Ta Ray Sa this is pretty strong shit," he said. "I don't think you should have too much of it".

I laughed, "Okay, I will go easy."

I took a few hauls of the joint and it wasn't long before I felt its effects. My head was already feeling a little light due to the drinks at the hall, and the pot made it feel even lighter. Things were going in slow motion and the heat from the seat below my ass made me want to melt further into the car. I could hear the music on the radio playing but I couldn't make out the song. The Russian and I just sat still for quite some time, not making any moves to leave the car.

Some time had passed as we sat stoned in the car listening to tunes and so I told the Russian, "We are paying for a hotel so we shouldn't pass out in the car."

He laughed and shut the engine off. Walking back into the building, all I kept thinking about was how I had hoped we would stay awake long enough to have sex. Sex was always the end goal with the Russian. Our relationship hadn't reached any kind of deep level, and so without the sex, the night would have been such a waste.

The Russian kept me from falling over as we stood waiting for the doors to the elevator to open. He pulled me inside the mirror lit box and as the doors closed, kissed me passionately. My head was light and spinning from the weed we had just smoked but that didn't stop me from enjoying the ride. I loosened the button to his jeans and pulled his zipper down slow as he continued to kiss me on the lips. His one hand was holding my face while the other had reached around and was on the back of my neck behind my hair. I nudged the Russian against the mirror wall as the elevator continued to climb higher. Moving my mouth from his lips, I started kissing his neck while reaching my one hand down into his pants. Opening my eyes once again while in the elevator and taking a quick glance at the sexy Russian fueled my desire to keep playing even at the risk of someone joining us. The Russian didn't seem to mind, either. His hands made their way down my back and he grabbed tightly on to my ass. With his cock in my one hand, I heard the elevator ding and the door open.

We made it to our floor and without anyone seeing our foreplay. I quickly pulled him out the doors with the waist of his pants in my hands, moving backwards along the hallway to our room. Smiling at each other, we knew that it was only a matter of minutes before we were going to be inside our room, ripping each other's clothes off. Fumbling for the room key, the Russian laughed as I continued to distract him by putting my hands down his pants and kissing his neck.

The door opened and we practically fell into the room, slamming the door behind us. As soon as the door closed, I pushed the Russian up against it and yanked his pants down to his ankles.

I wanted this man and I didn't want to wait any longer. I was pleased to see his cock was already hard and waiting for my mouth. As he stood pressed up against the wall, I went down on to my knees and grabbed his shaft with my right hand. Cupping his balls, I then placed my mouth over the head of his erect penis and played with it in my mouth. I heard him moan. He placed his hands on top of my head and held on to my hair, pulling it slightly as I moved my mouth further down the shaft of his cock; sucking and releasing the pressure with my lips as I did.

"Ta Ray Sa," he moaned as I continued to suck. "You don't have to stay down there on your knees," he stated. But I wanted to. I wanted the Russian to feel like he was the man of the hour and I was his whore. As I played with my mouth around his balls and kissed him in between his thighs, he grabbed a hold of my hair harder. I liked when he tugged it a little. It was turning me on knowing that he was super excited. The juices flowed from his cock and I could taste the salt on my lips. He was going to cum and I was going to let him.

"Ta Ray Sa, you suck me so well!" he whispered as I continued moving my mouth up and down the shaft of his penis faster and harder. I took the tip of his cock and made sure it reached the back of my throat, having all of him inside my mouth. Holding on to his ass with one hand and cupping his balls with the other, I felt the Russian

KELSON J

explode in my mouth. He groaned and moaned as he did, and I swallowed all of his saltiness.

The Russian helped me up from my knees and took my hand as he walked me over to the bed. Standing beside the bed, he held my arms over my head as he gently lifted my blouse off me, tossing it to the floor beside him. He reached behind my back and undid my bra with his one hand while he caressed the cleavage of my chest with the other. I heard my bra land on the floor beside my blouse. Taking his lips, he then kissed my mouth once and led his wet lips down the side of my neck, up to my ear, and back down to my neck again. Still cupping my breast with one hand, he then brought his mouth down my neck to my exposed nipple. Swirling his tongue around my excited nipple, he undid my leather pants with his other hand as his mouth made its way down to my navel. I felt my pants slide off and my panties soon followed. His mouth wasn't far behind.

With both hands cupping my naked ass, the Russian brought his mouth down to my waiting pussy. He shoved my body towards the bed, and I laid down on to my back, legs hanging off the bed. The Russian pulled my legs open and spread me wide enough for his face to make its way to my pussy. I had been anticipating this moment for some time, hoping that the Russian enjoyed eating pussy. As his tongue opened the parted lips of my vagina, I quivered and grabbed a hold of the bed sheets with both hands. His tongue continued to swirl inside me and my body rocked in excitement. His mouth was driving me insane and the high from the weed was intensifying everything I was feeling. I grabbed a hold of his head with both my hands and pushed his face further into me. Moaning, I felt him suck my clit and then tease me by taking his lips and kissing me between my thighs before he would return to my impatiently waiting pussy. The more he dove his face into me, the tighter I held on to his head and the harder I pushed him into me. Every cell in my body was tingling as this man continued to fuck me with his tongue. I let go of any worries in that moment, of any fears I may have had pursuing a relationship with the Russian. I didn't think about my Italian at home wondering what I was doing or me wondering if he was wondering about me. I didn't care that the Russian was much younger than me or that he knew nothing about my life before him. I let go of all insecurities I had surrounding my body, or the secrets I had, and just enjoyed the moment when the Russian allowed me to cum in his mouth.

The next morning the Russian and I woke up feeling a tad hung over and hungry. Having forgotten half my toiletries when I packed in haste the night before (I was too busy worrying about sending sexy selfies to my Italian), I decided to shower and make do with what I had. A hairbrush and elastic were the two main items I had neglected to bring. I struggled to pull through my wet hair with my fingers and had told the Russian how I was going to be embarrassed going down to the swanky hotel restaurant with my hair askew. He smiled at me and said, "I have an idea. Here let me help you." He then took a twist tie that had been used to wrap an electrical cord for one of the lamps, and twisted it into my wet hair, piling it in a bun of sorts on the top of my head. As he stood half naked behind me, his warm body touching mine, I faced the mirror before me. I smiled at him in the mirror as he carefully took his time to twist the tie around my wet hair. *He truly is stunning to look at,* I thought. I still couldn't believe this man who was so much younger than me wanted to have sex with me. My hand reached around and held on to his thigh, and soon I felt his cock get hard. As it was pressed up against my ass, the Russian started to kiss the side of my neck, his hand reaching around and grabbing a hold of my breast. Playfully he pulled at my nipple and rubbed the side of my breast sending shivers through my body.

Our bodies were both standing facing the mirror, my head cocked to the side, allowing the Russian to kiss my neck and shoulder and then my back. He was so passionate as he kissed me all over. I opened my eyes and enjoyed watching the sexiness unfold before me as his hand then went from my breast to my anticipating vagina.

He reached inside me with his fingers, spreading my lips wide as his big hand played with my pussy. I held on to the chair in front of me for support as it became harder to stand still. Every fiber in my body was enjoying feeling the Russian's fingers playing with my clit. As he continued to kiss the back and side of my neck, I watched in the mirror. Seeing his sexiness displayed before me was really turning me on.

My hand reached behind me to grab a hold of his firm dick. It felt so nice in my hand as I slid my palm up and down faster and firmer with every touch his hand made inside of me. I heard the package open as the Russian took the condom and slid it over his cock. Moving me from the grip I had on the chair, to where the bed was, he bent me over and slid his throbbing, hard penis inside me from behind. As he pushed deeper and further into my pussy, he still played with me with his fingers while his other hand held on to my ass. This drove me insane! As I gripped on to the bed sheets and let the flood of ecstasy take over, I heard myself moan, "Oh God!"

The Russian thrust his cock deeper into me over and over again as my moaning got louder and the grip on the bedsheets got stronger. We came together in a moment of sheer pleasure. When the Russian was done, I turned myself over and lay on the bed on my back looking up at him as he smiled, walking towards the washroom. I heard the shower turn on and I thought to myself, *now that was hot!*

We went to breakfast not long after our impromptu romp, my hair still wet and piled on top of my head with only a twist tie holding it in place. The restaurant was quiet and well-lit with big windows down one side of the room. We sat at a table for two by the window and ordered much needed coffee. The Russian was always so quiet with me and I felt oddly quiet as well. Our communication only seemed to blossom when we were fucking each other. Idle chit-chat bounced between the both of us and my mind wandered to another time in my life as the Russian relived our night before. I tried to pay attention to him but was taken aback when I saw a part of my past walk in through the door that lead to where we were sitting. Smiling awkwardly, I knew I couldn't ignore who was walking toward me. I jumped from my seat to greet him when he walked up to say hi. A quick hug was exchanged, and a flood of memories embraced me. I didn't introduce the Russian to who stood before me. I think I forgot he was even sitting at the table. It was so odd seeing him in the restaurant, a restaurant I had never been to until this morning. It was crazy that it had been fifteen years since we were last together. And it was odd that it felt as though it was just yesterday.

He smiled and said, "It was great seeing you."

I watched him walk to the other end of the room to catch up with his group of friends who had been way ahead of him. I didn't speak, I just smiled as I watched him go.

The Russian looked at me and quietly said, "You run in to people everywhere we go."

I replied, "Funny isn't it?"

CHAPTER 5

Sophia

The music continued to play loudly all around us. Sophia was having far too much fun. She was dancing around me and toying with the men that surrounded her. I was trying my best to look like I was enjoying myself, but I kept glancing back towards the bar where I had last seen my Italian and the Russian. I was wondering what was happening at that bar as I could no longer see the men. Were they speaking to each other? Had they come together? Did they both know I was going to be at the bar? Why were they here? All these questions raced through my mind while the music pumped in my ears. The dance floor was vibrating and there were people all around us, so it didn't surprise me when I felt a hand grab my arm.

"Sophia?!" I shouted as I turned around.

I met Sophia when she first came to work in the hair salon. Jessica, the owner, had brought her on and told me that she thought her talents would be appreciated by our team. She said we needed to bring a new vibe to the space and Sophia was just the vibe she was looking for.

She was super bubbly, loud and even a tad annoying at times. I remember thinking how very different we were, with her long bleached blonde hair, her very expensive and rather large boobs, tiny waist and small ass. She seemed so carefree, so confident, fun and full of energy, and I didn't like her. I didn't want to like her.

I was a prisoner in my own life at that time and Sophia represented everything that I was not. She was a reminder to me of who I had wished I could be. How was it even remotely possible that the two of us could work together, let alone become friends? Be we did. I tried to stay out of her way at first, and stuck within my comfort zone, but she wouldn't have it. She pestered me day in and day out with stories about her love life, or about how much fun she was having being single and I was jealous. It wasn't long before she knew about my situation at home and it wasn't long before she hammered it in my head that I deserved better and that I no longer needed to enable bad behaviour. I began looking at Sophia with a different set of eyes and I envied her. I wanted to enjoy life and not go to work every day feeling trapped and so alone. The more I got to know Sophia, the more her influence became the thing that helped free me from the shackles I had been chained to for so long.

The first couple of times Sophia and I went out, I wasn't quite sure what to make of her. She seemed to effortlessly put herself together while I was stalled in the washroom for what felt like countless hours just trying to get my hair or makeup right. She would laugh at me and say, "Ter, you look fucking great! Single life looks hot on you, so let's fucking go!"

She would talk to just about anyone. Men and women would hit on her in the bar, while I stood back sipping my drinks, watching from the sidelines. I often questioned myself in the beginning, wondering what the hell I was doing going out with her? I couldn't compete with that level of confidence, of sexiness. I had as much confidence as a mouse had going for that lowly piece of cheese in a trap. Sophia didn't seem to notice that I was a nervous wreck while out, or at least she never let on that she did. She would grab me by the arm, drag me out to the dance floor, or push me towards a hot guy standing at the bar and tell me, "Just go fucking talk to him!" Her persuasive pushiness, or what she liked to refer to as her "ball busting encouragement," often came with a bit of a price. I quickly found myself in situations that I wasn't prepared for. Sometimes the alcohol would get the best of me and Sophia would have to drag me back to the apartment we now shared and put me to bed, or sometimes I would find myself sneaking out of the bar alone to make it home before she did with one of her picks from the night.

Often, she would say, "I found the perfect guy for you!" I would cringe when she would go get him from a table and walk him over to where I was standing to introduce him to me. Mine and Sophia's taste in men were quite different. I learned early on that she didn't have a type. If they were fun and made her the centre of their attention for that evening, then they were her type.

I envied her. She didn't care what people thought about her. She was a square in a round world. My entire life, I always worried. I was a people pleaser. I never stopped to ask myself what I wanted, and I never gave myself permission to tell the men in my life what I wanted, or even what I didn't want! And because of that, I found myself attached to men that took advantage of me, men that put their needs above mine.

The more I hung out with Sophia, the more I began to realize that I, too, wanted to be that square in a round world and that I needed to stop trying to fit the mold of what everyone thought I should be. That part of who I was, that part of my old life, my past, was quickly dying and, like a butterfly that emerges from a cocoon, I was emerging as a woman who was longing to spread her wings and fly. Sophia was showing me how to. She was telling me that it was okay to fly.

CHAPTER 6

The Promise

T he grip on my arm got tighter and I turned to see it wasn't Sophia's hand I was feeling! Surprised wasn't the emotion I was feeling as I looked up from the hand on my arm to the bluest eyes I had ever seen. It was my Italian! My Italian was standing there, on the dance floor, and he was holding my arm! I was in shock. This was not how I had envisioned our first meeting to be.

"What are you doing here?!" I yelled.

Smiling, not saying a word, he gently pulled me away from the floor toward the washrooms. I was in so much shock that it was hard to resist following him. Lights from above were flashing everywhere, music was pounding in my ears, and all I could think of was that my Italian was holding on to my arm. He is here! I was screaming inside my head. He was in the bar where I was after all this time! Fuck! He is here in the bar?! And so is the Russian!

Jesus! I thought. *This isn't happening! This can't be happening this way?!* I continued yelling in my mind.

My Italian continued to push past the crowds of people all the while, never saying a word. He held on to my arm as he continued leading me off the dance floor and into the men's washroom. He opened one of the stall doors and nudged me inside, closing the door behind us, locking the latch. We were now face to face and tightly squeezed into a small space. My heart was pounding. It felt like it was going to come out of my chest! Men were coming and going into the washroom. I could hear the muffled music from the club as the washroom door opened and closed. Still, my Italian didn't speak. He just stood there staring at me. He looked me over from the top of my head, down to lock his eyes with mine, to my lips and then my neck. He let his hand off my arm and raised it to my cheek, touching it gently as though to see if I was really there with him.

I closed my eyes and shivered with his touch. His hand was smooth. He held on to my cheek and as he did, he moved his body closer to mine. My breathing intensified. I couldn't move, nor speak. I was still in shock. His hand then moved from my cheek and his forefinger touched my mouth, his finger run slowly along my upper lip circling back down to my lower lip where it then stopped. I opened my eyes to see him smile at me. I took a deep breath. I felt like I had been holding my breath since that stall door closed behind us and I worried I might pass out.

As he leaned his lips closer to mine, we heard the door to the washroom swing open again and this time two men came in. As one spoke to the other, I almost fell over. That voice! It was his voice! It was the voice of the Russian thanking the other guy for showing him where the can was. *How the fuck was this happening?!* I thought, freaking out. How was I locked in a stall with my Italian, a man I had been longing to meet and sleep with, while the Russian I had been screwing was on the other side of that door?!

I gasped. My Italian knew by the look on my eyes that I was quietly panicking. He smiled at me some more as he leaned closer towards my mouth with his. I closed my eyes again and took a deep breath. I felt his lips slowly touch mine. He kissed me so softly and before I had a chance to react, he opened the door to the stall quickly closing it behind him, leaving me standing alone wondering what the fuck had just happened. And yet this didn't surprise me at all!

Shocking, surprising, alarming, mysterious, infuriating, demanding, all words I would use to describe my Italian. The request to see me giving the Russian a blow job just topped the cake as one of the more shocking requests my Italian put before me. It had been weeks since my botched attempt to give him what he was asking for and he wasn't backing down. Almost daily, he would text, "So, when are you going to suck cock for me again?"

Initially, I thought he was joking, maybe this was a part of his kink to think he could get away with the request but he didn't really expect it of me. But the more he asked, the more he made me feel like he was daring me. I kind of liked it. I wanted to feel as though I was in control of the situation and so I made the promise once more telling him, "I am a woman of my word and I will get you what you are asking for."

"You promise?" he urged.

"Yes!" I replied.

I wanted to see how far he would take this request. Did he really want to see me sucking the cock of another man? When we would discuss what our online relationship was becoming, he told me, "I like you. Why do you question that? I like when you're being naughty for me and wanting to please me," he would remind. Or he would say, "Soon, we will meet. I told you that." I wanted him to keep his promise and so I thought if I either drove him crazy enough, or made him feel jealous enough, then he would agree to a date with me. And so, I made another date with the Russian, but this time it was for my Italian.

During the weeks that would take place in between my dates with the Russian, my Italian and I would heat things up on the phone. A day wouldn't go by that I didn't wake up thinking about messaging him or a night where I wouldn't want to hear from him before he went to bed. My mind would start to race with thoughts about my Italian and what he was doing when he wasn't texting or talking to me.

I would think about how he spent his time in the city when he wasn't on the phone with me. Did he go out to dinner with his friends, have women on his arm? Do they hold his hand or touch his knee? Does he look at them, cock his head to the side as he does in his photos to me, and then smile slyly at them? I wondered if my Italian took his women home with him. Did they get to kiss his lips or sleep in his bed? Do they make him breakfast the next morning, only wearing his dress shirt, or worse, did he cook them breakfast? Are there coffee dates, a trip to the movies or a play? I wondered, did the women visit him at work, pop by to bring him lunch, or call him up on the phone whenever they wanted? Did they get parts of him that he hadn't allowed me to see yet, I wondered? And I wondered while he was in the city, and not on the phone with me, did he wonder what I was doing?

I wanted to ask my Italian all these things, but I was fearful that I would push him away. He would tell me in a text, "I share more with you then I do with most." And on one particular night he did just that. He showed me a glimpse of who he was. As always, our steamy time on the phone ended with "normal conversation." I loved to hear his voice, it's so soft and sexy and yet has a take-charge energy of which he uses often in our play. We shared stories that night about our past experiences and we laughed. It was a playful energy he possessed that evening even after the steaminess of his kink died down. I really liked hearing him this way. While our messages back and forth are often filled with pictures of each other in the flesh, this time he was filling my phone with pictures of his work. I knew he must be an amazing artist by the way he talked about his work, but once he shared those photos, I fell deeper into who this man really was. There were so many layers to him and this night he was allowing me to peel back one of those layers, exposing a part of something he loved. And I was beginning to love him for that.

I enjoyed those rare moments with him. Most days, he would go back to being mysterious, aloof, even a bit pissy and demanding. He would frustrate me to no end, but I still wanted to impress him, to please him and to have him want me. Never had I wanted a man more!

Damn him, for letting me in and pulling me close and then pushing me away!

While on the phone, lying in my bed, I would investigate his photo with my eyes. My mind would trail to thoughts of how it must feel to have my lips touch his neck, chest and stomach. My nose would breathe in the warm scent of his cologne as my hands gently slid over every curve of his biceps. I'd let my fingers glide down his chest and rest them at his navel as the wet lips of my mouth would make their way to his throbbing penis. I could feel his excitement build with every touch my mind imagined. As I closed my eyes, I could hear him moan with pleasure. I would take in all that his photos had to offer me, and I longed for the day when my mind no longer had to do the imagining, but my body got to take over.

I learned quickly that his sexual appetite preferred more mystery, more dirtiness, and more kink. He would ignore me (or so I felt) or be quiet with me when things became too every day, too mundane and so I would try to pull him back with what I knew best when it came to my Italian. I would give him what he wanted. I would tease him with thoughts about me sucking the Russian's dick, thoughts about how my Italian was going to feel when he finally saw proof of me doing so. And I would keep him engaged by always letting him know that he was my main objective.

So, I told him that I had given the Russian a call. My Italian enjoyed hearing, "The Russian is gearing up for another hot night with me and looking forward to me sucking his cock again!" But before he came, Sophia and I had hatched a plan to get my Italian revved up for my big date. She picked up a bottle of red and brought it to the salon for the end of our shift.

"It will help us better concoct a plan to

keep the Russian happy and your Italian interested!" she laughed. Her calculating mind always amazes me, just as much as her beauty. Often, I wished I was gifted with the natural sex appeal she possessed. I mean it doesn't hurt that she's tall, blonde, works out like a fiend and has a rack that most men drool over! She is also intuitive, perceptive, and she helps me to see through the reserved exterior of the Russian, all the while helping me to tear down the walls my Italian has up. And the first step in doing just that was to stage a one woman photo shoot whereby I had enough sexy and very revealing photos of myself to send to my Italian on the day of my date with the Russian. All day long, I planned on not giving him a chance to catch his breath. As the wine was poured, the two of us joked that we are a force to be reckoned with, and we laughed that neither men had a clue. Sophia loved the game as much as my Italian did. She thought it was great that I was playing with him and she thought it great that the Russian was helping to play the sexy game. She kept telling me, "It doesn't matter what your heart is feeling, or that all of this is new to you! You were drowning, Ter, for a long time, and this is what is going to help you swim to the top!" She tells me that, "It's okay to live a little, Ter! It's okay to be selfish! It's okay to have fun!" as she pours me another glass of wine. "Promise me you're going to have fun with this, Ter!" she demands.

"I promise," I tell her. And I meant it.

The day of my date with the Russian was filled with excitement. I was looking forward to seeing him, but especially excited to spin the wheels of my Italian. He enjoyed the photos I sent him all day long – pics of a partially exposed breast, the side of my ass in sexy panties, my lips puckered just for him, my hand resting on my nipple or a glimpse of my thigh where my it met my pussy. I made sure to blow up his phone with these pics all day long. And he loved it! I got replies saying, "MMMM," or, "Tease!!" and, "Sexy!" But as the day got on, my Italian started getting more excited for what he called, "My other pics you're going to send me that you promised." I knew what he was talking about, and once again I began to feel nervous. He seemed adamant that he wanted me to this time follow through on my promise to get him pics of me sucking the Russian's cock. Once again, I wondered if I could go through with my promise.

The Russian came to pick me up for our date, this time taking me to a new wine bar that played live music in the downtown core. When he walked up my driveway, I saw the tall, manly features he possessed. I had forgotten how sexy he was dressed in his dark ripped jeans, black hooded sweatshirt and black leather jacket. His look was finished off with a black cap on his head, exposing his mysterious eyes and rugged, yet clean shaven goatee. The look was really working for him.

I greeted him with a smile, not showing him the reservations I was feeling earlier that day and secretly trying to not show him the effects of the wine I had shared with Sophia. We gently gave each other a peck on the lips and a quick hug. How I longed for that smell, and it was there, it was back! Oh, how I could have melted into his arms as soon as I smelled his fresh, warm laundry. I didn't realize how much I had missed it, as my Italian had a way of distracting me and my thoughts.

I think he was nervous, too. It had been a few weeks since we last saw each other, and as usual, he had neglected to return my text messages or show me any indication as to his interest in me. The Russian can come off as very cold or disinterested in his messages but once we are sharing the same space, our bodies become very interested.

We drank too much booze that night. The drinks were flowing, and the music kept playing. The Russian rested his hand on my knee, and I kept thinking about how amazing he smelled. I had no doubt in my mind that when we made it back to my place, the sex was bound to be amazing as the electricity between our glances was creating many sparks. I decided it was time to let him a little more into my world by inviting him for the night. It had been too long in between our dates and my Italian had revved me up for weeks. I had been looking forward to the date, not only because I longed to see the Russian, knowing he was travelling out of country for two months, but because I had entertained the idea of following through with my Italian's dirty request, and keeping my promise to him. His kink demanded, almost begged, to see photos of me in play that night and I was wanting to give that to him. And while I wanted to grant my Italian his sexy wish, I was also very apprehensive about doing so. Something felt wrong about it and with every drink I consumed, my guilt followed.

I would sneak off into the ladies' room and snap a photo to send to my Italian enticing him with every text about what he was missing out on by not being there with me. He would come back with responses like, "Keep going!" and, "You look amazing, my sexy slut!" This angered me! Why wasn't he jealous?! Did he really want to see me sucking the cock of another man?! Did this idea not enrage him even just a little bit?! It did me, but confusingly so, it also excited me more than I had expected.

The Russian and I left the bar that night quite fucked up. I barely remember getting into the Uber. Flashes from my phone filled the car as the Russian and I made out in the back seat, all the while I took photos to send to my Italian. "You look good!" he would reply. Or, "Fuck, you're sexy!" I would see on my phone through the fog in my eyes. The Russian didn't seem to notice I was checking my phone. I don't know how I even got away with any of it. Maybe because he would never imagine this scenario to be true?

We made it to the front door of my apartment, and as I fumbled for my key, I announced, "If you want the best blow job you've ever had, you will follow me to my room!" The Russian was not far behind.

I don't remember his clothes coming off or how we even made it to the bed. The room was spinning as I felt him pull me into him, motioning for me to make my way down to his hardened cock. My boots were still on and as I struggled to kick them off, I heard him say, "Keep them on, it's sexy!" *Fuck it!* I thought. *I can do this with boots on as long as I don't have to stand!*

The room continued to spin as I flung open the drawer to my nightstand. "Where the hell is it?!" I questioned.

I knew the cock pop rocks were in there somewhere as I had just bought them the day before. Stumbling in the dark with my one hand in the drawer and the other one resting on the Russian's chest, I felt him undo my bra. My bare breasts now exposed, and the Russian fondling them. I found the packet I was desperately searching for in the dark. As I ripped it open with my teeth, I asked him if he was ready for my surprise.

He moaned and replied, "Of course baby!"

I wet my lips and poured a small amount of the candy into my mouth. The popping and crackling surprised me a little. I had never used them before and was taken back by how sweet but intense they were. *Surely, he is going to enjoy this!* I thought.

As my mouth went over the head of his cock, I remembered my promise to my Italian. *Am I really going to go through with it?! Can I?* I wondered.

I withdrew my mouth, searched for the Russian's face in the dark and asked, "Want to take my picture, baby? Want to show me how hot I look while I'm sucking your cock?"

The Russian was surprised but didn't hesitate. He grabbed my phone from the nightstand and instantly asked me to pose (as any good photographer would) as I went down on him again. I looked up as the room spun some more and I gave the best sexy blow job face I could give. The flash went off and off and then off some more, and all the while I sucked the Russian until he came in my mouth. And then it was done. There was no going back now.

I don't really remember sending those pics to my Italian or the angry exchange that followed with them between he and I and how my jealousy for a man I hadn't met yet showed. Instead I enjoyed the rest of that drunken night with the Russian. After all, he was the one who was with me in the flesh and he was the one who, after that messy blow job, suggested we take a shower.

I lead him down the hall from the bedroom to the bathroom and turned the shower on. Climbing in together, we let the water wash the sticky mess from my mouth and his cock. As the warm water trickled between us, I enjoyed kissing his chest and stomach. It was exciting to feel the water rushing around us and our wet bodies touching each other. It was liberating for me to feel so open with him. I wasn't thinking about how my body was looking to him, but only enjoying the moment. He leaned his body back towards the shower nozzle so that the water flowed evenly over both of us. I made my way down to his cock with my mouth and heard him grab the curtain rod for support. His wet and now clean penis tasted great in my mouth and it wasn't long before the Russian was hard again. Grabbing on to his ass with my hands, I let my mouth play on his cock for a while until I felt he had enough teasing.

As I stood up to greet his mouth with mine, he moved my wet hair from my face so he could kiss me passionately while he was cupping my breasts with the warm water flowing between his fingers. The space in the shower was small and it made our time more intimate. I enjoyed running my wet hands up and down his bare chest to his stomach and gripping on to his slippery cock. We played like that for a while and the passion became more intense as our hands moved feverishly over each other's bodies and our mouths followed.

The Russian was more excited than I have seen in the past. He forcefully turned my body away from his, having my back now touching his chest. His hands cupped both my breasts and fondled them while his mouth kissed my neck and down my back. The water was all around us, making the energy between us feel hotter. He bent my body forward and let go of my breasts as he spread my ass cheeks apart and thrusted his penis into my virgin ass hole. I was pressed against the shower wall with my arms outstretched and my slippery hands holding on for support. The excitement grew when he placed one hand into my crotch and played with my clit while he thrust his hard cock inside me. Faster and faster and harder and harder, the Russian pumped as my hands slipped along the wall. The water continued to pour all around us as we soaked the bathroom floor. We enjoyed this position for a while even though it took me by surprise. Maybe it was the alcohol or maybe my newfound sexual liberation I was feeling, but I questioned nothing in that moment.

Even though I was hot from all the excitement, the water was no longer touching my body and I was beginning to get cold. I told him, "We need to take this back to the bed where we can really fuck."

He agreed as he pulled his cock out of me and turned me to face his wet body. Kissing me passionately, he asked, "Ta Ray Sa, I really want to fuck your ass again. Will you let me?" In all my years of having sex, I had never had a man do that before. It was never really something I had thought about, but in that moment, my only thoughts were on having fun with the quiet and now surprisingly dirty boy Russian!

We stepped out of the shower, and together we ran, dripping wet and intoxicated, to the bedroom. The Russian was right behind me, grabbing on to my wet ass, gently pushing me on to the bed so the fucking could continue. With my hands and knees resting on the mattress and my ass in the air, the Russian inserted his hard cock into my ass hole once again. I let him do what he needed to do to cum as the bed moved from one end of the room to the other. The sheets were already stripped from the bed and our wet bodies were now beginning to be covered in sweat. The Russian was enjoying this new treat of his.

I was glad Sophia was not home, because with the amount of noise we were making, she would have woken up for sure. As the Russian came with all the force he could muster, he didn't forget about me. He flipped me on to my back, spread my legs open with his hands and dove his face down in to my sore yet still welcoming pussy and ass hole. His tongue that night was the best I ever felt from him. The alcohol loosened him up as it did me, and I enjoyed this side of the Russian.

I forgot about my promise to my Italian. I forgot about how only an hour earlier, I had been sucking the Russian's cock and having photos taken to send to my Italian for his pleasure. I was just enjoying the Russian and everything he was offering me. He was in rare form that night as he was enjoying the new liberated me and all the benefits my Italian had imposed on him. I had forgotten about past promises to myself about only sleeping with men I was in love with. I was only in that moment remembering my promise to Sophia and to the new me I had become. I was keeping my promise of having fun and not worrying about anyone other than me. And I liked it!

The next morning, I rolled over to see the light on my cell phone blinking. With my eyes half opened, and a migraine from hell, the Russian's arm draped over my back, I swiped up to see it was a message from my Italian letting me know that I was going to regret how I behaved last night after he read what I sent him!" I read that text three times over trying to comprehend what he was saying and then a flash of memories entered my mind and I thought, *Oh shit!*

CHAPTER 7

The Aftermath

Left hanging. That's always been my Italian's M.O. And that's just what he did after he walked out of the stall. He left me hanging. I stood there for a short moment, trying to catch my breath, knowing full well how close I had just come to finally being with my Italian and how close I was to the Russian having been in the stall next to me. I was so turned on by what had just happened, and still surprised, nonetheless. To have both these sexy men that I had been enjoying in the same bar I was in meant that I couldn't let a moment like this pass me by. Confused by my Italian, I needed some kind of reassurance I was still desirable, and I knew the Russian, when pressed could give me that reassurance. So, I quietly snuck out of the stall and quickly opened the one next to me, knowing full well that the Russian just may be as surprised to see me, just as surprised as my Italian always keeps me.

For two days after that fateful night whereby I shared my most intimate moments with the Russian for my Italian, things were stressful. The argument with my Italian started as soon as I said my goodbyes to the Russian.

Text after text, we argued over how I felt sending those pics were wrong and how he felt my behaviour by getting drunk and tearing into him wasn't sexy. He told me that I had better not do it again. That pissed me off! His condescending attitude was often more than I could handle. He had this way of making me second guess my attraction to him and yet at the same time make me desire him even more.

How is that a man I didn't even know, that for some ungodly reason I actually liked, could have this kind of fucked up control over my feelings?! I wondered. How was it that he could anger me and yet still turn me on?!

I was feeling as though he was toying with me, letting me in once in a while and then pushing me away whenever it suited him. He got what he wanted from me, and yet I was no further ahead with him. He seemed to get a thrill out of seeing how far he could push me. And yet I found I still wanted to please him. I was enjoying the game, the kink even when I would fight with my inner morality, my desire to always be in control.

I told him, "I won't send pics like that ever again, so don't fucking ask me!"

He replied, "LOL, talk like a lady."

"LOL?!" I questioned. "How can you laugh at me right now?!" I demanded.

Silence. That's what my Italian does when he doesn't want to answer a question, or he answers me back with a fucking question of his own.

We argued over those photos and my night with the Russian for two days. And for two days, I was getting nowhere with my Italian. If he was any other man, I would have told him to go fuck himself and ended it right there, but every time he would push me away, I would feel the need to pull him back in. I was beginning to enjoy the challenge and I wondered if we weren't more alike than I wanted to admit. I continued to let him think he was in control, but I decided it was time I took some of that control back.

As I began to discover who I was as a woman, I decided I wasn't going to let anyone stop me. And I made no room for explanation or judgement. I decided in those moments of frustration with my Italian that I was going to live my truth and be who I was, as authentic as I could, and if he or anyone else didn't like it, they too could go fuck themselves!

And so, I called him on his bullshit. After two solid months of texting back and forth daily, countless nights sexting, and yet he still hadn't given me any indication as to when we would finally meet. This had me rattled. This, and his strong desire to push me towards other men. And so, I asked him, "Are you fucking married?!"

"Married?" he replied, "Never have been! Unlike you!"

Why he felt the need to throw that in my face, made no sense to me. He didn't know me back then, nor have we ever talked about that part of my life.

He asked me, "Why do you keep asking me that? I told you I am not married!"

Once again, he made me mad. "You don't want to meet me!" I typed. "You pick and choose when and how you reply to me." I stated and then admitted, "Because meeting you has always been my end goal, and right now I feel as though you are hiding something from me!"

"Soon!" He laughed. "Don't ruin things!" He demanded.

And then there was silence on the other end of the message for some time. I sat there staring at my phone, getting angrier by the minute. And finally, "Well, I told you at some point we would meet. But I'm not going to constantly keep explaining myself to you. You believe what you want! I'm going to bed." And then he dismissed me.

I screamed into my pillow and tossed my phone onto the nightstand.

Fuck him! I thought.

Fuck him! I don't need him! I don't need any of them! Sophia was right. I just needed to get out of my head and have fun. I needed to stop thinking so much.

I was so angry in that moment that I

thought I needed to find a release for my anger. I tried to masturbate. *Surely that would take the edge off,* I thought. I tried everything I normally would enjoy: the use of my middle finger playing with my clit, my finger deep into my pussy while I pushed down hard on to my hand; I even pulled out my vibrator. Nothing! I played with my nipples, while picturing my Italian's face in my mind, repeating his name over and over again, crying, "Fuck you!" But nothing was working.

I began to wonder if my Italian had broken me. I felt broken below the waist as my vagina was now thinking like my brain and all my brain was thinking about was how hurt I was feeling over my Italian's dismissive attitude towards me. I needed the Russian to come home. I needed him to come fix me. But he had already left the country and was going to be away for two months. This pissed me off further. And so, I did what any scorn woman in my position would do. I made a date! I made a date with another man. And I texted my Italian and told him so.

This time, it wasn't on his request. This time, he wasn't the one in control, and this time I was going to choose what I would share with him. I devised a plan in my head on how I was going to handle this date with a new guy and then I went to sleep, knowing that the next day, my Italian may or may not rise up to the occasion.

CHAPTER 8

The Cuban

Y ou can't stop the train once it starts!
That became my new motto and one I was living by the night I came face to face with my Italian and the Russian. I swung the stall door open just as the Russian was turning around to zip up his pants. He looked startled to see me standing in the men's washroom.

"What are you doing in here, Ta Ray Sa?" he wondered. "I followed you in here," I lied as I pushed myself in to the stall. He smiled, as did I. I turned to lock the door behind me.

I wasn't always so assertive. In fact, I was always more of an enabler, a pleaser. I was discovering that I could still be a pleaser if it also pleased me. My Italian, even through his arrogance and my frustration with him, was teaching me that. I was beginning to find my voice and was willing to share it with him and the Russian, on whichever day one of them was annoying me the most.

Things changed with my Italian and I after our epic fight. He was less apt to message me right away as was I to message him. I had decided he needed to be kept in his place and that was a place of still desiring me but without me giving him exactly everything he wanted. I toyed with his kink knowing he liked to see what I was wearing, and to hear who I was going out with. I challenged him by telling him about my upcoming date with a new guy. He of course played it off as though he was excited for me by saying, "What are you going to wear for him?" and, "Will there be cock sucking on your date?".

I sent him pics of what I was going to wear and asked him how I looked. Of course he replied, but this time with, "Great," and not his usual, "You look sexy," or "Beautiful as always," comments. I could feel he was feeling jealous and this made me happy. This made me look forward to my coffee date with the Cuban I had met online only days earlier.

The Cuban and I had exchanged some flirty text messages while I was feeling ignored by my Italian and missing the Russian. He was unlike any other man I had met. Not very tall, but certainly what he lacked in height, he made up for in stature. His body was amazing! He looked like he was built to last with his thick muscular thighs, his round tight ass, six pack abs and strong tattooed arms. In fact, I lost count with how many tattoos he was sporting all over his body and I didn't care because they all were working for him. His hair was shaved short even though he had shown me pictures of when he had once sported dreads that made him look like the twin to Lenny Kravitz. He had a full, thick, but short shaved beard, full luscious lips and super dark eyes. He was damn sexy and he knew it!

He wasn't shy about showing me his sexiness over texting or shy about complimenting me on my "...tight pants that looked good on my sexy hills." I would laugh at his messages because his accent was certainly coming through and his culture for the Latin life was showing. This excited me. He was a man who owned his sexiness and a man who wasn't afraid to tell me he desired me. And unlike my Italian, he wasn't willing to wait to have me.

Our initial meeting was at a local smoothie bar. The Cuban wasn't in to drinking coffee or alcohol. He took care of his body. I was nervous but really looking forward to seeing him in person, and I was looking forward to making my Italian jealous by doing so. I sent him a quick text, "Waiting on the Cuban," to which he replied with a thumbs up emoji.

When he walked into the smoothie bar, I swear I smiled from ear to ear. How was it possible that this amazingly fit, and stunningly gorgeous man was interested in me?! I questioned. I knew it wasn't going to be long before I coined him, "Amante," meaning lover. I wanted to have sex with every part of his dark-skinned body. And he knew it! He had been revving me up to the idea all week! He was a force to be reckoned with and was giving both the Russian and my Italian a run for their money. With the Russian's wish-washy ways and my Italian keeping me at bay, I entertained the idea of Facetime with the Cuban only days before our date.

The Latin lover was quick to take my lead after I had sent him a very strategic pose of my bare legs with a slight angle on my panties. He followed up with a similar pic of his well-hidden and seemingly large cock. Another pic of me, this time with my legs open and just the top of my white cotton panties showing, was followed up immediately with his hard, black, well exposed dick. I looked at his photo several times in amazement before replying; noticing his hand cupped at the base of it and still having room for another two handfuls of his penis exposed. It was such a turn on!

His thick Caribbean accent comes through in every text, and while I understood all he was saying, it took away a little from the horniness we were feeling. He must have felt that too or maybe he was just more experienced in the world of online dating than I was, and so he requested we do things over Facetime. I panicked for a minute, similar to how I once panicked when my Italian typed those two little words, "Call me."

I was in my panties and a t-shirt, hair disheveled, and I no longer had any makeup on. How could I look and feel sexy over Facetime with this extremely muscular, hot, dark-skinned, luscious-lipped, tattooed, Lenny Kravitz look alike?! I feared.

I tried to make an excuse as to why that wouldn't work, saying Sophia was just in the next room, but he wouldn't have it. He was very persuasive with his sexy accent in text and his very alluring photos. I turned the lights low and then he called me.

"Hello, Mami," he whispered. "You don't have to talk. Let me show you what I want to do to you," he said.

He looked yummier than I had imagined or how his photos portrayed him.

"I like that skin you show me, and your thickness," he moaned as he gripped his very large cock. "You make me melt with curiosity when I look at that sexy shape of yours and your round ass in those panties," he smiled, still rubbing his cock. "I would like to be right now in between those legs of yours with my mouth, making you feel so good," he continued.

I started to get wet hearing him say those words. I turned the camera of my phone down to my crotch to show him as my hand made its way in between my white panties. "Mmm, that sounds like that would be fun!" I told him as I rubbed my clit.

"I can feel your hand pushing my head

against you while you let me eat your pussy," he said, "and eating that nice ass of yours making, your body go crazy," he told me.

I replied saying, "You did promise me that you know how to please a woman, right?"

"Yes, I said it and I meant it," he promised. "To look at those legs and that smooth skin makes me melt right here that all I can think of is eating you non-stop," he motioned as he brought his mouth and his full lips towards the camera to mimic kissing me.

I was getting hornier with every word he said and I enjoyed watching him stroke his hard cock in the camera.

"I'm so horny and you turn me on big time with that thickness and that edible ass of yours, Mami. You have no idea how much of a fire you have put on me!" he said. "I haven't touched a woman in a long time, and you have me crazy and my blood is extra hot for you, Ms. Beverly Hills."

His words and seeing him stroke his cock got me so excited that I forgot I was holding my phone. I would move the camera closer to my pussy so he could have a look while I, too, watched him play with himself. Hearing him speak to me while he did was such a turn on. I remember thinking, "Why haven't my Italian and I used Facetime?"

"Are you feeling wet while you're touching yourself?" he asked me. "I wish to feel that ass and that pussy right now! It feels so good my dick is getting crazy hot!" he told me. "I want to cum for you, Mami, and I want you looking at me cumming," he begged.

"Show me," I whispered, hoping Sophia wouldn't hear me. The more he showed me, the more I anticipated seeing him cum. My hand was having fun in my pussy and my mind was racing with how crazy and hot I was feeling. This complete stranger was making me cum, and I was enjoying every minute of it!

And so, when he walked into the smoothie bar, it was hard to not think back to that hot night over Facetime, making me blush a little when he walked up to greet me.

"Hello, Mami," he said as he walked up towards me. "How's my baby doing today?"

I smiled, knowing just how this night was going to end.

"I'm excited to see you," I told him.

He smiled back. "That's good to know Mami, because we are going dancing!"

I wasn't really dressed for a night of dancing, but the Cuban, my Amante, didn't seem to notice. When he spoke to me on the way to the bar, he would lean over from the driver's seat and gently touch my hand or my arm with his fingers. He was animated. Loud. And from what I could tell in the ride to the club, he was going to be fun. He filled our time on the drive telling me about his time in Cuba as a young boy, his distaste for tequila and his love for his family. His stories were intriguing, and they made me laugh. I couldn't stop staring into his mysterious dark eyes that seemed to look right through me. Surely this guy knew how hot he was.

When we got into the club, the music was already lively. People were milling about from the bar to the dance floor and the energy was electric. I reapplied my lipstick on the car ride and messed up my hair a little, hoping to fit in. When the Cuban wasn't looking, I quickly undid the top button of my blouse, revealing the well thought out bra underneath. I have learned that a girl can never be too prepared for when a hot date night might appear. And this night, I was grateful that I had shaved my legs and waxed my pussy.

The Cuban grabbed my hand and lead me to the dance floor. Watching him move and sway his hips to the music was enticing. He had come dressed in black jeans that tapered at the ankle, Nike runners, a black and white stripped, long sleeved shirt and the sexiest black bowler hat. A black leather jacket adorned his well chiseled body. He wasn't a drinker but we each had a beer and I a couple shots of tequila to take the edge off. Having him move his body closer to mine as he danced made me more and more excited. Our eyes didn't leave each other. We touched each other's bodies as we swayed to the music, him having his big hands resting on my ass or around my waist as he nuzzled his mouth into my neck. Even though the dance floor was packed, we didn't notice. He kissed me on that dancefloor and when he did, it was with an intensity I wasn't used to. Not normally one for public displays, I didn't care that I was standing in the middle of a dancefloor with a hot Cuban man, making out. The more he kissed me, the more I fell into a trance. "Do you want to leave?" I heard my lips ask.

"Yes, Mami, let's get out of here." He gestured as he took my hand and lead me out the front door.

The word passionate doesn't describe the Cuban's lust for the female body enough. Words like devour, intensity, hunger, erogenous, and stimulating make the cut. Sex with him is raw, is animalistic, hot! He told me he was holding back our first time, and this surprised me, excited me and scared the hell out of me!

As I lay in bed beside him the next morning, I couldn't help but watch him sleep and relish in the beauty he possessed. His body truly was a temple. He was chiseled in all the right places. I had never had sex with a man who took such care of his exterior (quite the opposite really). I felt lucky, even a little guilty and not deserving. His abs seemed to go on for days and I enjoyed the feel of them very much. His ass was hard as a rock and a delight to hold on to. The tattoos that covered his skin made his sexiness come to life even more.

I remember fondly holding on to his strong, defined biceps when I was sitting on top of him with his rather large cock inside my very welcoming pussy. Feeling the strength of them under my hands made the ride all the more enjoyable. He didn't let me hop on top right away and take control as I was used to in the bedroom, whispering, "Not yet."

I reached from the bed to turn off the side table lamp, but he stopped me, insisting, "Keep it on! I want to see you!" He was a man who knew what he wanted, and he wanted me to enjoy all he had to offer me!

As we peeled our clothing off layer by layer, the Cuban kissed every inch of my naked body, starting with my mouth and ending with my toes. He had enjoyed the play we exchanged with our eyes in the club earlier that night – my gift for temptation and flirtiness – but once our bodies hit the sheets, this Latin lover took over and was in control!

His hands were all over me and his mouth always followed. I knew he had waited all night to really dig in and grab a hold of my ass, his favourite part of my body. His hands grabbed on tight and squeezed my ass as his mouth made its way to my anus. I had never had a man go there with his tongue before and while he did talk about it in the week leading up to this night, I was still shocked. The sensation wasn't at all what I was expecting. It wasn't bad but it wasn't what I was used to. His experience in it was definitely noticeable, but I have learned through some of my recent trysts is that for me the most excited I get is when a man has his tongue sucking my clit. And luckily for me, the Cuban knew how to do just that!

As he flipped me over on to my back from my previous kneeling position, his mouth went right for my hot and anticipating cunt. I lay back with my arms stretched behind me, holding on to the headboard as he fucked me with his beautiful, full lips and amazing tongue! I was in complete ecstasy as I orgasmed over and over again! Grabbing a hold of his head, I pressed his mouth deeper into me and cried out in euphoria!

I had to beg him, "Please stop! I can't take anymore!" as my body shook and my mind was going insane. He didn't listen. He didn't stop! He just kept fucking me with his tongue and allowing my juices to flow into his willing mouth.

We made our rounds around the room that night as the Cuban noticed my dresser situated across from the end of my bed. With the lights already on, I was feeling a tad intimidated by the Cuban's amazing body paling in comparison with mine. I joked earlier in the week, "I think you're too damn sexy for me!"

He laughed replying, "As long as you don't lose that booty Mami, we will get along just fine!"

Standing in front of the dresser, fully naked, the Cuban asked me to "bend over baby so I can grab a hold of that beautiful ass of yours."

I leaned my body forward and placed my hands atop the dresser, staring at my disheveled hair and sad looking makeup in the mirror. The Cuban was standing behind me, now rubbing his hands up and down my back and over my ass as he watched himself in the mirror. He looked hot doing it and he made me feel even hotter. All my insecurities went away as he thrust his cock into my pussy from behind. It was so much bigger than I was used to, and it took me some time to warm up enough to really let him go deep.

With each pump he made, he went deeper into me, staring at me and himself in the mirror.

Remembering my promise to my Italian, "You like to watch yourself?" I asked. "Grab my phone and take some pictures!" And so, he did. The flash went off a few times as the Cuban continued to fuck me harder each time. I held on to that dresser as much as I could, feeling my hands slip and move each time he thrust himself into me. I reached my hand behind me to motion to him to hand me the phone saying, "Here, let me take a pic from this angle," when I noticed the red light on the camera indicating it was recording. "Are you videotaping?" I asked surprised.

"Yes, Mami, we are looking hot!" He moaned and smiled.

I smiled back at him, thinking My Italian is going to love this!

The next morning, I was woken up with the Cuban rubbing his dick against my ass. Barely having had any time to sleep the night before, I was surprised he was rearing to go again so soon. His hand went up into the t-shirt I had thrown on before we passed out and he was now playing with my nipples. I was so tired from barely sleeping and my body ached, but all I could think was, damn, that was a good night! I was hurting all over, having felt like I had run a marathon, and I didn't think my body was capable of taking any more on, but the Cuban was persistent and I was enjoying it.

It wasn't long before he had me wet and while half asleep, I was now begging to be fucked. I threw a condom at him from my side of the bed as he flipped my body over on its side and spread my ass cheeks apart.

"You're too big baby," I told him. " I don't think I can handle that," as I knew where he was intending to put his hard, enormous cock.

"Shh, Mami," he motioned as he spread me wider and licked his finger. Inserting it into my ass hole, he played to lubricate it as his cock followed not far behind. It wasn't easy at first and unlike with the Russian, it hurt a little, but he was as gentle as a guy could be with a cock his size.

Moaning, he kept pushing it in further and further, yet slowly. I started to enjoy the feeling, having only done anal sex once before with the Russian. This time, the Cuban knew enough to place his fingers inside my pussy as he pumped to help me orgasm. I learned the night before what a pleaser the Cuban was and how his main objective was to make me cum over and over again before he took his turn. He didn't cum in that moment. Instead, when he knew I had, he pulled his cock out from my ass and lied back on the bed, motioning for me to hop on top. Now he was going to let me climb on board and ride him until he came, and I was determined he and I were going to enjoy every moment!

Lowering my body on to his throbbing cock felt so good! As I rode up and down, he demanded, "Look at me." We stared in to each other's eyes intensely as I continued to ride him, getting wetter with every minute. He would kiss me periodically and hold my face to stare into his eyes with the smoldering look of a man who meant business.

"Fuck! You're so hot!" I moaned. "I'm going to cum!" I cried.

I could see the look on his face changing and I moved my body over him faster and harder. He started to close his eyes.

He grabbed me close and held on to my back with both arms wrapped tightly as we pressed our bodies so close to each other, both of us cumming at the same time. It was fucking insane! I loved it and I was afraid of it. Where did this guy come from? How was it that only a week ago he was a new Tinder match and today I was getting my brains screwed by this man who oozed sexiness? I questioned. I lied back on the bed trying to catch my breath. Feeling relaxed and exhausted, I thought to myself as I looked over at him, shit, I hope he doesn't ghost.

CHAPTER 9

Veronica

"Hey! Ter?! You in here?!" I heard them call. "Ter! You fucked off on me and I saw you sneak in here!" It was Sophia and it sounded like she wasn't alone. The Russian looked at me and laughed under his breath.

"Shh! Damn!" I whispered. "I have to go. I have to let Sophia know where I am, or she will be worried. You understand?" I asked. "Let me get rid of them and I will come back for you. Promise. Just don't stray too far!"

"Of course, Ta Ray Sa, go. I will catch up with you later," he said.

Still shaken from my hasty encounter with my Italian and feeling anxious from being face to face with the Russian after all this time, I walked out the stall to where my friends were waiting.

It wasn't a surprise that it was Veronica who was camped out in the men's washroom with Sophia when I stumbled out from the stall. Veronica was always game for anything and Sophia told me she had called her when she saw that I may need some help.

Veronica was one of the clients from the salon. Sophia and I had become good friends with her. She was on board with my plan to help me keep my Italian interested and to help me tease him.

She texted to ask if I would take boudoir photos of her. She knew I enjoyed amateur photography and she wanted to celebrate being a woman by showcasing the parts of her body that she loved while trying to fall in love with the ones she didn't.

I told my Italian about my steamy request and he got excited. He asked, well almost demanded, to be a part of the process. Secretly, I knew by mentioning this to him that this was the bait I needed to keep him interested in me and to keep our kink alive. I couldn't think of any man who wouldn't get excited at the thought of two women together and so his initial response when I mentioned it wasn't a surprise.

"Is your friend as hot as you are?" he asked.

Typical, I thought laughing.

"Why of course she is!"

Veronica is hot, beautiful really, even though she doesn't know it or believe it. She's a heavier girl with curves in all the right places and God gifted her with amazingly large breasts and a killer smile. I predicted my Italian would find her appealing with her full lips, delicate nose, bright green eyes and deep cleavage. I felt honoured that she had asked me to take her photos, knowing full well that I wasn't a professional photographer but that I enjoyed snapping pics. I had already filled her in on my new love for the racy boudoir style photos I was sending to my Italian.

We planned the sexy photo shoot as a surprise for her new man, but now that she knew that my Italian was also excited about it after having shared the idea with him, she was geared up to help me play a little. I actually think she was more excited than I was.

"So, when are we doing this Ter?!" she shouted. "I can't wait to get these guys of ours all riled up!" She laughed.

The day was set, and my Italian wouldn't leave me alone about it. He would text asking, "Are you looking forward to taking pics of your friend?!" and, "Will you be joining her?" I would laugh at his schoolboy interest in our photo shoot, but play along with his kink to see me half naked – hell, possibly even fully naked, posing alongside Veronica.

"Yes, of course I'm looking forward to it," I told him. "I want to make my Italian happy," I typed, knowing full well that this is what he wanted to hear.

Earlier in the week, I helped Veronica pick

out some sexy lingerie to wear for the photo shoot while we shopped at a local store. The two of us came out of the change rooms like teenage schoolgirls excited to show each other what we were trying on. I was sending photos to my Italian with my choices, enticing him further into the idea of posing alongside Veronica in her pics, while she was at the same time sending photos to her man. We would giggle and laugh about how these guys were eating up the tease that we were dishing out.

"Wait till you check out his responses, Veronica! He's eating these pics up!" I giggled from the changeroom beside hers. "He can't wait for Sunday!" I laughed. "I'm not sure who he's more excited to see in the pics, me or you." I shouted.

The salesgirls helping us must have thought we were crazy but we didn't care. Veronica and I were having so much fun and I was having fun showing her how freeing it felt to not be confined to how society says a woman should behave. And I was enjoying seeing Veronica coming out of her shell as I had once done not long ago with the help of Sophia.

My Italian was so excited for the photo shoot. In fact, he drove me a little nuts leading up to that day.

"Will I be allowed to watch?" he would plead. Or, "Will I have a hand in the poses?" He was relentless. I told him that I would allow him to have a hand in the process, all the while, Veronica and I agreed to play it up just for him. The game was far too fun not to play because my Italian was far too easy to entice. He was anxious to jump on board, even if it was only from the screen on his phone.

I allowed him to imagine the prospect of Veronica and I getting even closer than just friends during that shoot. I liked how our texting would get hot whenever he asked about the photoshoot. He would throb whenever we would talk about it.

"Are you going to pose naked with her?" he would ask.

"Maybe," I would tease.

"Are you going to kiss her?" he would question.

"Maybe," I would tease again.

"You're going to touch her breasts?" he would wonder.

"Maybe," I would laugh.

"And her pussy? Are you going to kiss her pussy?"

Jesus, he drove me nuts about it! But I kept playing along because I knew in the end the kink and our time on the phone would be worth it. And I was always longing for our time on the phone.

The day had finally come, and Veronica came over to the apartment early. Sophia was already at work, so it was just the two of us, a bedroom, sexy lingerie, and my Italian. He was easily accessible that morning. I noticed how quickly he would return text messages all week leading up to the "big day."

I was excited. I was excited for Veronica because this was a step in the right direction emotionally to loving herself. I was excited to help my friend see just how sexy she really was, and I was excited she was going to let me play with my Italian at the same time.

There were many costume changes that day. Changing in front of each other became comfortable quickly with the idea of running around my bedroom half naked while I was snapping pictures, pictures of Veronica strewn across my bed, holding a vibrator for effect or a glass of wine. I would pose on the bed beside her, showing her some of the sexier poses I had already perfected for my Italian when we would play. We would giggle at the thought of how silly some of them made us feel all the while knowing that once taken and edited, they were going to make the men in our lives really horny.

My Italian, as predicted, was texting while I was snapping photos. He wanted us to get down to the real nitty gritty, asking me, "When are you going to lose the bra?" and, "Are you going to send me pics of your sexy friend posing with you?" So, with Veronica's permission I fired off a few safe pics to my Italian of the two of us posing in our sexy lingerie. He was pleased, responding with, "You ladies look delicious," and, "I want to see you kiss her, will you do video for me?"

Up to that point, I had wondered how far

my Italian was willing to see me go. I mean, I had already sent him a photo of me and the Russian and video of the Cuban and I, and so I wondered, wasn't that enough? I began to realize that his sexual appetite was a big one, and in order for me to keep him engaged, keep him interested, I needed to up the ante. He even goaded me saying, "I knew this was all smoke and mirrors!" That pissed me off! I couldn't let my Italian know this was just a game I was playing with him. I needed him to believe that I was willing to take things as far as he wanted me to. I needed him to go crazy with lust for me, to want to follow through with his promise to want to "fuck the shit out me" when I drove him crazy enough. After all, that was my end goal and I wasn't going to fail at my quest to have the one man that I couldn't have easily. And so, when I approached Veronica with the idea of us taking our bras off and posing face to face half naked with each other, she was game.

"Let's do it!" she shouted. "Let's give your Italian a show!" I was nervous. I had never been in a situation like this with a woman. I was enjoying exploring my sexual desires and not apologizing for them, and while the idea of being with a woman had intrigued me, I wasn't sure how I would feel if the opportunity actually presented itself.

Veronica was far more comfortable then I was. Losing her bra easily, she was ready to pose in any position I thought would get the Italian all hot and bothered. With that, I had to also agree to let her send some of these pics to her man. We climbed on to the bed after we had set the camera on a timer. Facing each other, we started posing with our breasts touching each other's. Nervous laughter filled the room as we smiled at each other and at the camera before us. I suggested I touch her one breast so that my Italian didn't think we were just playing with him. It was an odd feeling in that moment. Veronica was a good friend and so the attraction to take things further just wasn't there, but I had wondered if she was a woman I had just met how I would feel. I needed my Italian to believe this kink and that just for him, and I was willing to go the distance. And so, we posed together, and I snapped away. Staring in the camera, I imagined it was my Italian's eyes I was staring in to. Picturing him looking at those photos and getting turned on by me was turning me on. I couldn't wait to hear his reaction.

The pics I sent him he raved over. "Fuck, you ladies look hot!" he texted. "My cock is throbbing!" he typed.

I knew it wouldn't take much. I got excited knowing that later that night, my Italian was going to want to play on the phone with me. I knew that we would use Veronica and the photo shoot in our kink, and I knew I would tell my Italian just what he wanted to hear to get him to cum for me. And for me to cum with him.

As I had hoped, my Italian and I played again

that night. The photo shoot with Veronica was just the foreplay he needed. He likes the chase and likes to feel like he's winning the race. He relishes feeling as though he is in control of the relationship between us. So, on this day, I gave him what he wanted. It had been awhile since we had some fun over the phone. He, being too busy with work commitments and falling asleep in the middle of our texting (joking his age was showing), or me being preoccupied with messages from the Russian while he was away.

Our usual back and forth sexting took place as it often does. It started off with some banter about why I didn't have sex with Veronica and of course following up with a struggle for both of us to control the conversation. When I frustrate him just enough, and he messaged me saying, "You're a tease." I fired off a couple of sexy selfies with my shirt off or showing a glimpse of my panties. It wasn't long before he wrote, "Lose the bra!" and, "show me what I want to see!" I sent him a sneak peak of my pussy, and it wasn't long before he demanded the pussy pic with me holding a handheld mirror in place so he can see my face and my vagina at the same time. I sent him those pics willingly now. I don't worry whose hand they could end up in. As I rediscover who I am as a woman, I make no apologies.

He sent me pics back and forth of his hardening cock. It's a beautiful penis and I tell him, "I want to ride your cock!" I tell him that I imagine how much he would enjoy having me suck it for him. He loves hearing what I would do with him given the opportunity. The majority of our kink always involved someone else in the room with us. And this night, we played with the idea of that someone being Veronica, just as I had hoped.

It got hot and heavy pretty quickly, and it wasn't long before I saw the words "call me" come across the screen. I longed for him to type those words and anticipated getting more turned on by simply hearing his voice.

I lay in my bed with the lights off, candles lit and my phone to my ear. I imagine my Italian in the bed beside me as he tells me, "Close your eyes and imagine that I am caressing your nipples as Veronica is kissing your neck. You enjoy feeling her lips on your body don't you?" he asked.

"Yes," I tell him.

"Now imagine her kissing your lips as I make my way down to your beautiful pussy with my mouth," he whispered.

"Oh, I am!" I tell him, "I can feel your tongue inside me," I replied, now getting really turned on. My hand makes its way down to my damp panties and my crotch as I picture this hot scenario in my mind.

"Veronica is now playing with your sexy breasts and biting at your nipples," he continues, "I spread your legs wide, holding your thighs open with my hands and I am fucking your beautiful pussy with my mouth. You like that don't you?!"

he questioned.

"I do!" I tell him.

"You like pleasing me?" he asked.

"I do!" I whispered, getting more turned on by his voice and my hand in my pussy, my clit swollen and throbbing.

"You enjoyed taking pictures of your friend for me today, didn't you?" he asked me. "You wanted to fuck her for me, right?" he demands.

"I did!" I tell him. "I want to please you!" I said.

"Are you going to cum for me?" he whispered. "I want to cum for you!" I hear his breathing getting more intense alongside mine. It's hard to hold on to the phone in one hand while I play with myself with the other, but my desire to cum with my Italian is much stronger. I can hear him stroking his hard cock on the other end of the phone and I can see it in my mind. I imagine that he is letting me stroke it, letting me kiss his lips, all while Veronica is teasing my body with her mouth.

The play we had that night was more intense than the ones before. My Italian and I were a lot more comfortable with each other. I was more comfortable with him. No longer was I in my head questioning how "real" this relationship felt or how much longer was I going to have to wait to meet him. In those moments of togetherness, I felt the most connected to him. While our faces had never met and our bodies had never actually touched, I felt more of a closeness and a vulnerability to my Italian that I had ever felt with the Russian in the many times I had fucked him. I began to worry that I was getting myself in to some trouble. I began to worry I was falling for my Italian.

CHAPTER 10

The Waiting Game

I grabbed Sophia's arm and Veronica's hand, and the three of us went running out of the men's washroom, leaving the Russian all on his own.

"Was that your Italian in there with you, Ter?!" Veronica questioned. "Sophia texted and told me that both he and the Russian were here! You must be freaking out!"

Truth be told, I was freaking out. I had just come face to face with my Italian for the first time and it was cut short by the Russian walking in on us. And then my time with the Russian was cut short by the girls walking in. My head was spinning! I felt like I was playing a waiting game, a game I was all too familiar with. I needed a fucking drink!

I'd been playing the waiting game for some time now – pretty much most of my life, really. I found myself waiting for the Russian to come home, after being away for six weeks, to see if we could pick up where we left off. I was waiting for my Italian to say the word that he was ready to meet me, and I was waiting to see if the Cuban wanted to see me again.

The waiting game is one I have been a player in for as long as I can remember and one I've gotten really good at. I find myself always waiting on something or someone. Something good to happen, something bad to happen. Always waiting and always on something.

My marriage had been a waiting game. For years, I waited for my husband to love me the way I needed him to. I waited to feel like I was a sexy woman that he desired. I waited for him to see me for who I really was, for him to want to know the essence of me. And I waited far too long because that time never came.

I waited for the love of my life to come back to me, and when he did, I found myself waiting for him to get better, for him to choose me over his demons. And once again, I found myself waiting too long, because once again, that time never came .The waiting game was all I ever played and so when I broke free from the cycle of waiting, I decided that I wasn't going to wait for anything that wasn't deserving of my time.

I was hoping the Russian was worth waiting for. While he was out of country working, I decided that I wanted to wait until he came home to see where our relationship was going to take us. He would text me periodically, letting me see photos of his travels, filling me in on some of his daily adventures. With every pic he sent, I felt a little closer to the quiet, sexiness of the Russian that I once adored. The distance didn't seem to matter and the frustrations that I once felt with him in-between our dates had seemed to diminish.

Two months was a long time to be away from the dreamy Russian. I wondered if we could keep our flame burning with such a distance between us, but he was proving to me that the distance didn't seem to change things. He would tell me, "I can't wait to come home." With his quiet, Russian demeanour, I knew that he meant he was missing me.

"Do you miss me?" I would ask him anyway.

"Yes," he would reply with a handsome pic of his sun kissed face.

I began to look forward to my almost daily morning wake up messages from him. Sometimes it was just a photo of him or his work and other times it was simply a 'hello' to let me know he was thinking about me.

My days were filled with work in the salon, while my nights I waited to be distracted by my Italian. Sometimes, while waiting for him to message, I would lie in bed staring at an empty glass of wine that sat atop my dresser, waiting for messages to come into my phone. I waited for messages from the Russian while he was away and messages from my Italian who was looking to play.

Playing with both men at times could be fun. I would send one sexy photo to the Russian saying, "Thinking about you!" and send the same photo to my Italian with, "Missing you." Both men loved the visual and both men would compliment me by saying, "You're beautiful," or "You're gorgeous," and both would get hard-ons when they did!

But while I was waiting for the Russian to come home and for my Italian to show me that I didn't need the Russian to keep him interested, I grew tired of waiting. I wanted to text my Italian so badly. I wanted to tell him how much I was beginning to really like him, to want him. But I couldn't allow myself to give up that much control, to be that vulnerable. And so... I found myself once again waiting.

I wanted to play with him. But he didn't message me. My addiction to messaging him was strong, but I knew the chase was stronger. So, I didn't text him, nor did he text me. Instead for several nights, I went to bed waiting, alone, dreaming about him and hoping he would text me.

When I closed my eyes, I imagined his strong, manicured hands caressing my body. I could sense how the scent of his cologne would fill my lungs and pull me deeper in to him. He would brush my face with his palm and kiss my lips sweetly, making his way down to my neck. The tickle of his whiskers would make me laugh as his mouth trailed further down toward my chest. I would take a deep breath as he sent shivers up my arm, and my nipples became erect. I imagined my Italian lowering my bra straps with both his hands, exposing my breasts in wait for his mouth. The sexiness of his patience is what was turning me on the most. He wouldn't rush things, never did. He would look up from his crooked smile at me with his head cocked to the side, before he moved his face down on to my bare breasts. The air in the room would feel cool, but I was only feeling the warmth from the energy we were sharing.

As I lay back on the bed, my Italian would play with my nipples with his mouth and his hands. I could imagine that I would place one of my hands on top of his head and grip the bedsheets with the other. He followed my body with his mouth, down to my navel, gently kissing me around my belly button before he took his hands and slowly lowered my panties. More shivers raced through my body as I watched him take them off. Spreading my legs slowly, he would smile up at me. He liked to tease, my Italian, and he teased me with his eyes and his hands before his mouth entered my wet pussy.

Gripping the sheets stronger now with both my hands, I would rock my body in unison with his tongue. He would moan with me as he fucked me with his mouth. As I lay there, withering in ecstasy, my body climaxing with the thoughts of my

Italian, I was wishing I hadn't waited for him to text me. I was wishing I had texted him after all.

Those nights where I had so much free time to think about my Italian or miss the Russian became less and less as the weeks went on. It wasn't long before the Russian's return home and I began to wonder if my Italian was more excited than I was for his return.

"Are you looking forward to seeing the Russian after all this time?" my Italian would question. "Did you miss sucking his cock?" he would wonder. "I bet he missed that beautiful pussy of yours!" he would state.

"Do you miss my pussy?" I asked him. "Do I still make your cock hard?" I pleaded.

"Yes!" he would type back. "But you know I love when you suck cock for me!"

I would sigh to myself as I began to wonder how much more waiting I was willing to do before I wasn't going to wait anymore to be with him.

The Russian would be home soon, and I looked forward to seeing him and to finding out how much my relationship with him was based on my time spent with the Russian. And so, I waited.

CHAPTER 11

The Return

The music was so loud in the club that night, but all I could hear were the thoughts racing around my mind. The girls pulled me from the washroom and towards the bar on the far side of the room. My eyes were quickly scanning all the dark-haired men in the club and all I could think about was where my Italian had taken off to. Sophia was pulling me so quickly through the club, often knocking into people as we passed, but I couldn't find him in the crowd.

I was still in shock. What the hell was he doing here, I wondered, my mind being pulled in too many directions. Why, after all this time, did he come find me? Why now?! And where the fuck did he go?

I could feel my heart beating faster as we neared the bar. I needed to stop and take a deep breath, but the girls wouldn't let me. I hadn't even processed what almost happened between me and the Russian after all this time apart, either.

"Ter, you need to regroup!" I heard Veronica say.

"Yeah, shit girl, this is fucking intense Ter!" Sophia shouted.

"What the fuck are you going to do?!" they both yelled.

"I'm going to order a goddamn drink!" I shouted back. "That's what I'm going to do!"

Drinking was what the Russian and I seemed to enjoy doing when we were together. It was a kind of commonality that took the edge off of both of our quieter sides to our personalities, and opened the door to our more adventurous sides. And so, it wasn't a surprise that when the Russian came home after two long months away that I suggested we go out with a group of my friends and have some drinks. Of course.

Every time the Russian and I have distance between us, I always worry if we are going to connect physically the way we had before. However, this time was different. I had spent a hot, steamy, long night with the Cuban, and I was worried that he might have ruined it for the Russian.
Both men were very different. The Russian, quiet, sexy, and dreamy, as I mentioned many times before, yet also very distant and noncommittal. The Cuban, fun, feisty, passionate and damn hot! Also, not a man I could see myself connecting on any kind of emotional level with. I didn't want to compare them or their abilities between the

sheets. But how could I not? I questioned. The Russian was the first man I had slept with since becoming single and my times with him helped me heal my broken heart, even just a little. But the Cuban... The Cuban was different. He helped me come out of my shell, even more than my Italian had helped me with our many steamy, kinky nights on the phone.

I was actually feeling a little sorry for the Russian, and truth be told, a tad guilty. I knew he had big shoes to fill!

There was a new club that opened up, so the Russian and I decided to head there and meet Veronica, Sophia, and a few of Sophia's male friends. This was the first time the girls were meeting him, and I was feeling a bit anxious. I wanted them to like him, but more so, for him to like my friends. I knew that the Russian and I would never become more than bedmates, but it was important for the people in my life to at least see and understand the validity in my sexy decision to sleep with him without the need for a commitment, something that was new and foreign to me.

I knew Sophia would approve. She was my free-spirited friend who never felt she needed to rationalize her decisions, good or bad. And I respected her for that. My new-found freedom was allowing me to express who I was in a way that needed no explaining either and I was enjoying it. At times I worried that I might meet someone I'd fall hard for but in those moments with the Rus-

sian, I had become very good at compartmentaliz-
ing my feelings.

The club was cozy and quaint. It was a hidden bar promoted as a Speak Easy with live mu-
sicians playing jazz in the corner. The door to the
club was hidden down a dark alley off a side street
and only lit by a small overhead light. We knocked
a few times on the metal door before a gentleman
opened it demanding, "Password please."

We all laughed.

As we headed down the narrow cement
stairs to where the club began, I could feel the
Russian's eyes on me. For a man who didn't say a
lot, his words and intentions were often spoken
through his mesmerizing eyes and smoldering
stare. I smiled quietly to myself, knowing that his
intentions for a hot night were still on his agenda,
even after all the time that had passed between us.
The vibe between the group and the Russian was
really good. I was able to sit back and relax while
the drinks flowed. Everyone was having such a
great time laughing, singing along with the music,
eating food and getting to know one another. It
was nice to see the Russian in his element interact-
ing with people other than me. And while he did,
he still took the opportunity when he had it to
rub his hand along my thigh, place his palm on the
small of my back, kiss me gently on the neck. His
interest was genuine, and I was forgetting about
all the time that passed and the steamy night I had
spent with the Cuban only a few weeks earlier.

It wasn't long before the bar was closing and the group of us stumbled out on to the street. I could hear Sophia teasing the Russian about how much he had to drink shouting, "You know you're going to have whiskey dick now!" and the group erupted in laughter. I laughed, too, because the Russian never had a problem getting hard when we were drinking, but we really did drink a lot that night. I think he was trying to keep up with the other guys at our table.

Sophia left in a cab to spend the night out and so it was just the Russian and I heading to my apartment. When we got there, I remember feeling excited to show him the special surprise I had in store for him.

"You are amazing, Ta Ray Sa," he whispered in his thick Russian tongue as he watched me open the sex grab bag of goodies. "You always have surprises for me." He smiled.

I had been holding on to the bag of sex goodies for the past two months and was excited to see what was in store for us that night. The anticipation alone got my juices flowing! The Russian lied on his back, smiling up at me, with his one arm draped around my waist as I showed him with excitement what was inside.

"Oh wow! A cock ring!" I exclaimed. "Make sure you put this baby on!" I demanded.

He laughed nervously as I began to unzip his pants. I could tell the alcohol had taken its toll on him because he was horny, but he was having a

hard time holding his head up. He looked so delicious as he would lift his head slightly and lean in
for a kiss. The alcohol had taken its toll on me, too,
but I was determined to finish the night off right.
After all, somewhere in the back of my mind, I anticipated it could be the last sex-filled night we
spent together.

While it was true that we seemed to fit right
back in with each other after the time that had
passed, I realized that that time gave me the distance I needed to come to terms with how I was
really feeling. I had gotten swept up in my new-
found freedom, my sexual liberation, I guess, and
while I was having fun, I knew deep down the Russian was just there to scratch my itch. Sophia even
said as much.

As the Russian continued to rifle through
the bag, I was applying a tingling cream to both
my lips and his already exposed cock. The Russian, always comfortable in his skin, had already
striped his clothes off and was lying in wait before
I had even stumbled my way over to the bed. Getting him hard wasn't difficult, especially once my
mouth made its familiar way to his penis.

Tossing the bag aside, the Russian was
clearly no longer interested in its contents and
only in what my lips were doing to the head of his
now hardened cock.

While we were enjoying our time together
under the sheets, I found myself comparing the
Russian to the Cuban, something I didn't want to

do. Maybe it was the booze, but he was simply less passionate than he had been in the past. Kind of lazy, really. He was fully enjoying letting me take the lead, and while I often enjoyed being in control, I was missing feeling like I was the object of his desires rather than a means to an end.

I needed to turn things up a notch and remember my ongoing promise to my Italian to let him see my talents unfold. Grabbing my cell from the nightstand, I slid my body off the bed and away from the Russian. He was lying there a little dazed and possibly confused in his drunkenness.

I whispered, "Baby, you like when I suck your cock right?"

He lifted his head off the pillow slightly and smiled, moaning, "Yes."

Turning the video on, I passed him the phone. "Want to record me sucking your hard cock?" I motioned.

The Russian didn't hesitate. After all, he was a photographer, and this was right up his alley. He enjoyed being the one in control of the phone that night and I... Well I was the one in control of his cock. As the phone recorded my play with the Russian's penis in my mouth, I smiled knowing that he wasn't the only one that was going to enjoy seeing my lips on his cock. I gave it my all knowing my abilities were being put on display, but it was far too obvious that the Russian, while very much enjoying it, was having difficulties with his abilities.

He did try his best that night, given what he

had to work with. As I recall those moments now, I chuckle, thinking it was a bit of a wasted night. We hadn't had sex with each other for two months, and yet we chose to get so obliterated that in the end, neither one of us really had much fun. Maybe that was a foresight into what was to come for me and the dreamy Russian. Either way, I was happy I got to play with video again and yet nervous about how it was going to look to my sober eyes the next day.

After much determination on both our parts – okay, mine mostly – we passed out. I don't remember if I even came (disappointing right?!), but I know the Russian... Well, he did not. Whiskey dick definitely ruined our night. The Russian slept like a rock while I lay back thinking about the Cuban, wondering if I would see him again and wishing I could text my Italian to tell him all about the night, yet knowing when I did, I was going to have to make up something more steamy to satisfy his desires. I finally fell asleep confident knowing that at least I had the video to fall back on and I knew he was going to be quite surprised!

The next morning, the Russian woke up surprised by his hard on, but it wasn't necessarily the surprise I was hoping for. My head was pounding from the booze, lack of sleep, my hair disheveled, makeup running down my face. And yet, the Russian was now ready for his morning blow job. I felt compelled to give him at least that. After all, he gave me more than he bargained for with the video. Even though I was still left unsatisfied, and this was the first time the Russian left me like that, I felt I owed it to him. His return wasn't at all what I had expected.

CHAPTER 12

The Douchebag

"A vodka soda, splash of cran and three tequila shots please!" I shouted over the crowd hovering around the bar and the music drowning out the waitress.

There was a sea of people in the club that night as the girls and I fled to the bar along the back wall, hoping the Russian wouldn't find me easily. I was still reeling from the recent events from the evening, and I needed to take the edge off while I hid. I needed to figure out my next move.

"Down the hatch, ladies!" I screamed, lifting the shot glass in the air. "To my Italian, the Russian, and the fucking mess I'm in!" I declared.

As I tilted my head back and threw the liquid down my throat, warm breath tickled my ear. Taking me by surprise, I turned to see him smiling down at me. He touched my shoulder with his hand.

"Imagine running in to you here after all this

time!" I heard him yell.

"Imagine that!" I screamed back as I turned to Sophia and Veronica and mouthed the words, "Fuck me!"

It was D standing before me.

They say a good player never makes you feel like you're being played. I can attest that this is true. D never made me feel like he was playing me. In fact, quite the opposite. He had a way of making me feel like I was the only woman he could imagine spending his time with. Even when I resisted his advances, he still laid it on thick, telling me, "Why would I want to talk to anyone else when I'm really enjoying getting to know you?"

His charm was always enticing, and his bright blue eyes and dimple in his chin just added to that. I didn't initially want to meet D. He made me nervous, and not the nervousness you get from the anticipation of meeting someone new for the first time, but nervousness from meeting someone you could see a potential future with.

I wasn't looking for a man at that time that would provide me with emotional stability. Lord knows, with the guys I was entertaining, I was only looking for distractions, for fun. My Italian would remind me of this whenever I was getting the feels for him. But D's calculating sexiness began to sneak up on me. He infiltrated my head space in a way that made me forget about my Italian for long stretches at a time. I honestly didn't think that was possible, but with D, it seemed as though anything was a possibility.

And that's why it was so upsetting to find out that he was really such a douchebag.

Our initial contact was like the others: online. He was quick to message me as soon as we matched. Not typically my type with his fair hair and fair skin, but the dimple in his chin and the brightness of his eyes caught my attention. I scrolled through his many pics and gravitated to the ones with the facial scruff. He seemed like he could have many sides to him. Little did I know how true that was.

He looked oddly familiar and I had wondered if we had met before since he was local to my area. In my line of work, many men cross the doors of the salon and I just hoped he wasn't a client's ex-husband or boyfriend.

We were quick to exchange phone numbers, taking our conversations off the dating app, a process I had become all too familiar with. He filled my phone daily with adorable pictures of him and his daughter, his baked goods (damn, he looked yummy in his baking apron, sans a shirt!). His baking looked as sweet as his messages were.

I didn't share the idea of D with my Italian. I wanted what I was building with him to be kept a secret. I think because, somewhere down deep, I knew that this kind of relationship would make my Italian feel threatened in some way. While he entertained the idea of me fucking other men, I didn't think he would like it if I was having feelings for them. His narcissism allowed for me to only have feelings for him. He only wanted me to please him. And until I met D, I was enjoying doing just that!

D and I would chat for hours. He would make me smile outwardly, and I began to look forward to his messages more than I did my Italian's. And I wasn't missing the Russian as much, especially after our last mediocre night together.

D took my mind off things. It felt easy with him. I felt as though I could let my guard down, a mistake I hoped I would never make again.

During the time I was getting to know him, I was being pulled into the idea of settling down again. He would send me sweet messages saying, "I hope you love to travel!? I can see the both of us laying somewhere on the beach, just the sun, the waves, you by my side, and a drink in our hands."

I would chuckle at the thought, but somewhere inside me, that promise I made a year earlier to not allow my heart to be broken again was being forgotten.

"Where are you and I going on vacation?" I would ask. And, "How soon do you want to go?!"

He would type back, "You say the word and I'm all yours!"

We played like this for a few weeks while I still kept my phone open to my Italian. My heart, my mind, and my morality were pulling me in many directions.

I needed to meet D.

It was a Saturday night. I was going out with the girls and D had gently suggested, "If you want to slip away from your friends later, my door will be open and I will be waiting for you in my room."

His invite intrigued me. I had never done anything like that before. Did I dare show up at his house, without ever meeting him first, and crawl into bed with him?! Why the hell not?! I pondered. After all, we had made this amazing connection, and I felt he was the real deal.

Sophia, Veronica, and I partied like we always did. We consumed way too many drinks, danced way too long on the dance floor, and, like always, Sophia left the bar with one of her many admirers while Veronica hopped in a cab and went home to her man. I stood waiting outside for my Uber as I texted D. There was a part of me that was hoping he was already asleep and his invite to come over was all in fun, and there was a part of me that wanted to see this naughty side of me through.

My phone lit up as I was standing, waiting for my ride.

"I'm awake and I've been waiting for you, Beautiful. Sending you my address now. The door is unlocked. I can't wait to kiss those sexy lips and look into your stunning eyes for the first time."

My heart sank. This was really happening! As the Uber pulled up, I hopped in and without thinking, I gave him D's address.

D didn't live far from the club. In fact, he was

in a neighbourhood I was familiar with. As the car drove down the street making left and right turns, I was in my head thinking about how this first meeting was going to go with him. I mean, call it what it was – I was in a car on my way to have sex with a guy I hadn't even met yet. 'Holy shit!' was all I could think.

As the car pulled into his driveway, my heart dropped a little into the pit of my stomach. Every sound piece of advice I had been given growing up about the dangers of meeting strange men was no longer a thought in my mind. *Fuck it!* I thought. *I am a grown ass woman! Men do this kind of thing all the time! Why can't I? I told myself that I owed it to myself to throw caution to the wind and have some fun. That's what I had been doing this past year, anyways, so why should this be any different?* I wondered. That was the pep talk I was giving myself as I climbed out of the cab and walked up the walkway to D's porch and front door. Hesitating for a quick moment, I looked back to see the cab drive away.

I turned the handle of the door and it opened. Taking a deep breath, I walked inside the house. I slid my heels off and dropped my purse on a bench by the door. Taking a quick glance in the mirror to my right, I followed the voice who I heard say, "Baby, I'm just down the hallway and in the bedroom straight ahead." Soft music was playing and the hallway was dimly lit, enough for me to see where I was going. D had definitely taken the time to set the scene.

I followed his voice down the low-lit hallway to his bedroom. As I pushed the half-closed door open fully, I saw him lying on the bed waiting for me. I could feel the smile come across my face as I locked eyes with him and saw him motion me to come towards him. I was relieved. He was exactly how he looked in his pictures, even better in the flesh. My reservations were soon leaving me, and my confidence took over.

As I walked towards him, I began to peel the layers of my clothing off, dropping one by one to the floor. The room was dark and only lit by a few candles that flickered on a dresser nearby. The scent of lavender filled the room from a diffuser on his nightstand. I soon realized the music playing was from the playlist D had sweetly made just for me.

I climbed on to the foot of the bed, slowly making my way over his body but taking my time kissing him along his thighs, and inside of each of his legs, grazing my mouth over the bulge in his boxers. He continued to lay there, not saying a word to me but smiling the entire time as we kept our eyes locked on each other. My hand gently caressed his stomach, my fingers trailing up his chest as I felt his hands reach around to gently rub my back and arms. I felt him unlatch my bra, slipping it off me, exposing my breasts and erect nipples. My new liberation was really turning me on. With no words spoken between us, our eyes once again locked as I bent my face down to kiss his smooth chest. I allowed my tongue to glide over his nipple and make my way to his neck. Kissing him from one side of his neck over to the next as I now straddled his well-defined, six-foot-one body.

Not wanting to rush the moment but getting more excited, I reached down and slowly pulled off his boxers, exposing his hard cock. I was pleasantly surprised. Continuing to keep my gaze locked on his steel blue eyes, I slid my panties off, letting them hang out down by my ankles as I climbed on top of his penis with my pussy wet from anticipation. Lowering down on top of him slowly, I enjoyed taking in every inch, listening to him moan. My intent was to tease a little before we really got down to business.

It felt so good to feel him inside me, this stranger who I hadn't exchanged a word or a kiss with. I felt naughty. I felt like the sexy slut my Italian wanted me to be. And I was enjoying every minute of it.

That night was hot, not going to lie. When D and I first kissed, the scent of his cologne filled my lungs, and I felt as though his kisses meant something. I knew the second I saw him that what I had been feeling over the phone was real. He had this uncanny ability to make me forget the Russian and to make me want to forget my Italian. I got swept up into his kisses and remembered all the sweet things he had said to me over the prior weeks leading up to this one night. I could feel my heart softening. *Was he the one I was waiting for all this time?* I wondered. We continued to make love through most of the night, exploring each other's bodies while the candles lit our way and the soft music from our playlist continued to play. I felt as though my heart grew a little in that moment and I didn't want the night to end. Little did I know that after that night, my heart was going to be broken once again.

CHAPTER 13

The Disappearing Act

"What are you doing here?!" I shouted over the music. "You have some nerve coming to talk to me after all this time D!" I yelled. "I'm pretty sure the fact that you ghosted me after fucking me doesn't allow you that right!"

He smiled and locked his steel blue eyes on me.

"I've missed you," he screamed. "I was a fucking idiot!" he shouted back. I heard Sophia laugh.

"No, you're a goddamned Douchebag! Now why don't you go fuck off?!" she said to him sternly.

Veronica grimaced and looked away, her face in her hands. I shrugged my shoulders.

"Yes, D, why don't you just fuck off!?I don't have time for your ridiculous mind games right now! Maybe come find me after a few more of these!" I motioned to my drink in front of me. "I would have to be pretty fucking drunk to ever sleep with you again!" I yelled as I turned my back away from him, picked my drink up and took a big swig. I stayed just like that until he finally walked away.

After dodging that bullet, and throwing back several more tequila shots, the girls were once again ready to dance. As they dragged my drunk ass to the dance floor, I couldn't help but check out every dark-haired man we passed again. As I tried to get into the music and make myself look like I was having fun, I really only had one thing on my mind and that was finding my Italian.

The girls were having a great time with everyone around us. The reggae beat was smooth, and it wasn't long before I began to loosen up enough to get into the mood. The tequila shots we threw back earlier didn't hurt the matter, either. I was laughing and having a blast on the dance floor, yet my mind was still on my Italian. I wondered, *did he actually disappear for good this time or was he somewhere in the bar lurking and watching me?* He did like to watch after all.

I wondered if my moment with him passed as quickly as it had come.

And then I felt it. I felt the warm hands wrap around my waist from behind. *Holy shit!* I thought. Did he actually come find me on the dancefloor again? I quickly turned around, smiling, hoping to look once more into his devilish eyes. But I wasn't faced with my Italian after all. No. This time it was another familiar, sexy face, yet not my Italian's face. This time the man touching me was no stranger to wrapping his big arms around me. This time it was the Cuban who was holding on to me tightly and while shocked, I was happy to see him.

"Damn! You look good!" I shouted as I hugged him. "What are you doing here?" I questioned.

He slyly smiled at me.

"Mami, I saw your Facebook post. You checked in here and I thought, damn girl, I needed to come see my baby and feel that hot ass of hers again!"

I laughed. He was always so descriptive and definitely not shy with his words. Blame the bar lighting, the pumping tunes, the energy in the bar, the booze, or shit maybe the endorphins, but in that moment all I was thinking about was how amazing it would be to leave with him and take him to my apartment for one long, hot night of fucking!

"I'm glad you're here," I smiled. His hands still around my waist and his mouth lingering around mine. "You going to kiss me or what?!" I yelled.

The Cuban brought his full, sexy lips towards mine, and within seconds, his tongue was in my mouth. There we stood among the crowd on the dancefloor, once again making out like we had the first night we met. I got lost in that moment. Nothing was on my mind other than how fucking hot the Cuban was. But the feeling didn't last long. Sophia was shouting in my ear.

"Ter! I have to take a piss! Come with me! Now!" she shouted.

Fuck! I thought. Why the hell was she dragging me away from him? Didn't she know I wanted one more steamy, sex-filled Cuban night?!

I kissed him one last time and shouted, "Don't take off! I will come find you," as I was being pulled away off the dance floor by Sophia and with Veronica in tow.

"What the fuck Soph?! Why did you drag me away?! You know how fucking hot he is!" I was so pissed off at her.

She laughed at me. "Ter, you didn't notice? You didn't see who walked right past us and landed at the bar? Jesus, Ter, do I have to do everything for you?!" she wondered.

"I have no fucking idea what you are talking about Sophia. Veronica, what is she talking about?" I questioned. I think I was feeling the full effects of those shots now.

Veronica laughed. "Ter, he's here! At the bar, like Sophia said!"

"Who? My Italian?! Did you see him?! He's at the bar!?" I shouted back. I was once again freaking out inside.

"Jesus! No, Ter!" Sophia yelled. "Get your head out of your ass! Forget about your Italian for a second! HE is here! The one you like to call The Scorpion!" she giggled as she stumbled into me, hugging me and holding my hair in her hands. "Focus, Ter! You need to go talk to him!"

Veronica agreed.

I turned to where the girls were pointing and after a moment of trying to get my eyes to focus across the room, I saw him. I saw him in all his glory. *Oh my God!* I thought. How was it possible that this night was happening? First the Russian and my Italian walk into the bar together, then I run in to that jackass the Douchebag, the Cuban on the dancefloor and now HE is here? The Universe was playing some kind of fucked up joke on me. And I was beginning to wonder what it all meant. But looking at him from across the bar, all I could think about was how amazingly rugged and handsome he looked. I sighed, remembering our last time together, and then I remembered what they always say about a scorpion. They say they can inflict a painful sting. They won't kill you but, damn, it will hurt real bad!

My Scorpion did just that fifteen years ago. He was the first guy I had had the most amazing sex with! It was free of any kind of pressure or title. It was steamy, uninhabited, hot, exciting and young. And I never wanted it to end. But it did. Like all scorpions, they can become predatory. And back when I was with my scorpion, I was young and not wanting to settle down or be claimed by anyone. Kind of how I felt now. Full circle, they say. Whoever "they" are!? Ironic, however, that the one I did settle down with and marry turned out to be the scorpion's best friend and not the one I should have settled with at all.

So, you can imagine that I was taken aback the day I first saw him again after fifteen years. It was that day I was in the restaurant, enjoying breakfast with the Russian after our night of fucking. My heart was in my throat when he walked up to me to say hi just as it was when I ran in to him again at the beach while the girls and I were out for the day, only a couple of months ago.

I was heading to the snack bar to grab us some drinks when my scorpion came sauntering towards me. Smiling as big as he always did, oozing that scorpion sex appeal that I could feel in my pussy. He always had that pull on me.

"Hey, Ter, twice in a couple of months! How crazy running in to you here!" he said as I saw him look my bikini up and down.

It is crazy! I thought. What the fuck was the Universe trying to do? Didn't it know I had a lot on my plate with the on-goings with my Italian, the trysts with the Russian, shit the desire to hook up with the Cuban again?!

"Yeah, crazy is right!" I smiled back. "You're looking good. You've aged nicely," I joked.

He laughed. "That's because I don't have a wife that makes me fat!"

He always had a sly way of making jokes to pull me in as he flirted with me.

"I heard you got married!" I told him. "Lucky woman," I chuckled.

"Who the hell told you that?!" He questioned. "Not true," he lied, looking down on me with his chocolate brown eyes.

I smiled back, knowing he was full of shit but not caring either way. He was looking so good to me and I had thought about him many times over the years, even while I was married to his best friend.

"I'm camping out here with a few of the old gang," he told me. "My tent is just past those trees," he motioned, smiling.

Shit! I knew where he was going with that comment, and truth be told, I was okay with it. Flashes of the hot sex we used to have were racing through my mind and I was wondering if he was still as good in bed as he used to be. Hell, even the zodiac said we had the perfect chemistry, me being a Capricorn mate to his Scorpion stinger.

"Oh yeah?" I questioned. "And where are the guys now?" I wondered.

"They are at the beach bar getting their drunk on," he laughed. "I saw you walking up from the beach and had to come say hi," he said. "Ter, you look amazing! I've missed that sweet body of yours!"

I laughed. "I bet you have!" I joked back. "I bet you thought about my sweet body while you were sleeping with your wife!" I replied. We both laughed. He even got a little red in that very tanned face of his.

"Come on, Ter, don't be like that. You know

you were the one that I let get away! I've missed you. And truth be told, I'm separated. Come hang with me at my tent and catch up with a beer."

I laughed inside my head. I knew what "catch up" was implying. I looked back toward the beach to where the girls were sitting. Would they notice if I disappeared for a while? After all, it's just one beer, I thought.

Walking beside my Scorpion down the sandy path past the snack bar and through the woods to his campsite had me reminiscing about the time long ago when he and I had camped together and decided to go skinny dipping.

"Do you remember that time we went skinny dipping at the lake?" I asked him.

"Fuck yeah!" he laughed. "I remember how cold it was and that my balls climbed up inside my groin!"

We both laughed as we walked.

"I do recall that I helped warm them up" I chuckled and gave him a wink.

"Why, yes, you did!" he smiled. "And I loved every minute of that!" he winked back.

Jesus! I wasn't lying when I said he aged nicely. He still had a full, thick mane of dark hair, but now it was sprinkled with salt and pepper. His dark tanned skin from all his years of outdoor work and his love of golf glistened with the sun as we sat on top of the picnic table, drinking our beers.

"Damn, Ter! I can't say it enough, you look

amazing!" He smiled, leaning in closer toward me, his mouth close to my neck. "And you smell delicious," he whispered as his lips grazed my ear.

Shivers went down my arm and the hair stood on the back of my neck.

My Scorpion's electric energy was filling my body. I could feel I was losing my resolve. Thinking it may have been a bad idea to follow him back to his campsite, I said, "I should go now before we get ourselves in trouble," as I slid my ass a tad further away from him on the table, taking a swig of my beer.

He smiled at me and I thought, Oh damn, that smile! "Ter, you don't have to go. Sit with me a while. We have a lot to catch up on," as he moved his body closer to mine on the table top. His one arm now draped over my shoulder, his fingers touching my bare skin and playing with the thin strap of my bikini top, twirling it around his finger. "This bathing suit looks amazing on you, Ter," he said. "I've missed you. Did I tell you that already?" he whispered as he leaned towards my lips with his mouth.

"You did," I whispered back as I felt my hand slide onto his thigh without my permission.
"I've thought a lot about you ever since I ran in to you at the restaurant," he told me. "I got jealous, seeing you there with another guy. Is he your boyfriend?" he questioned.

I laughed, slyly replying, "Boyfriend? No, he is not my boyfriend."

He smiled, wide and as sexy and as sly as could be. I knew I was so fucking doomed.

"You were thinking about me?" I questioned as I felt my lips move closer to his. My body was betraying everything my mind was telling it. I was losing the battle and as I felt my lips touch his, I knew I was screwed! It felt as though no time had passed between us. That kiss was the most electric, passionate kiss I had ever had. It was the kind of kiss I imagined I would have the first time I kissed my Italian.

Sitting on top of that picnic table, kissing my Scorpion for the first time in over fifteen years, surrounded by trees and the blue sky, and all I could think about was how fast we could make it into the tent nearby before our clothes came off. But I didn't think quick enough because before I knew it, my Scorpion was helping my bikini top off as his lips were making their way down my neck.

The skinny straps to my bra slid off my shoulders easily and the piece fell to my waist. Sitting there fully exposed, feeling the breeze on my naked breasts felt amazing while my Scorpion's lips and tongue made their way to my nipples. Leaning back on the table with both my arms holding me up, I closed my eyes and enjoyed feeling him take each nipple one by one into his mouth. His hands soon followed as he grabbed my breasts, fondling each one while his mouth made its journey down to my belly. Laying fully flat on the table now, I opened my eyes for a brief moment to raise my head to look down at him.

His handsome ruggedness captivated my heart and his mouth captivated my pussy that was getting wetter by the second. Closing my eyes again, I continued to feel the breeze sweep across my nipples and the air blowing in my hair. Off in the distance, I could hear the waves crashing along the beach and the echo of people talking. The Scorpion and I were in our own little bubble. In that moment, nothing was going to interrupt our time. I had forgotten that the girls were probably wondering where I fucked off too. I had forgotten that I was half naked laying on top of a wooden picnic table, and I had forgotten that my Scorpion was still technically married. None of that mattered when I felt him slide my shorts off along with my bikini bottoms. Exposing my bare pussy to the sky, he spread my legs apart and his warm lips made their way to my clit.

Moaning and grabbing on to his salt and pepper hair, I let myself enjoy every minute of his tongue. He continued to eat my pussy as I remembered how good he was. Time had not escaped his abilities. My orgasm in his mouth was as intense as it had ever been. Feeling his lips on my clit and his tongue deep inside me had me orgasming over and over again as I pushed his head deeper in to me. Fuck! It was truly the best oral orgasm I had had in a long time!

The Scorpion eventually came up for air

and when he did, he gently grabbed my hand and pulled me off the table, walking me to the tent. Opening the zipper slowly, all the while having one hand touching my body, he led me into the tent. As I bent down through the doorway, leaving the flap open behind me, I watched the Scorpion remove his shorts. His cock was still hard from our time on the table and it stood waiting for me to put my lips on it. I walked toward him, fully naked, and helped him lift his shirt off his hairy chest and over his head. I missed that body. He was always such a physical guy. He played baseball, golfed, had a physical job working in the trades and it showed. For being an older guy, his age didn't show in his physique.

Staring down at his hard cock, all I could think about was how great I remembered it feeling inside of me. We both smiled slyly at each other as I walked toward him and kneeled on the floor of the tent. Luckily for me the ground was fairly level, and luckily for my Scorpion, I was anxious to suck his cock. It felt as good in my mouth as I remembered and as I remembered, my scorpion wasn't shy to tell me so.

"Mmm baby, I've missed this! You always knew how to suck my cock well!"

The Scorpion's cock was a fun one to suck. If I could ever say a cock was beautiful, his was! It was pierced and it was always fun to navigate around the piercing. I think the pleasure he got from it was because it hurt him a little, and he never complained when I took a little nibble on his balls or sucked a little too hard on his shaft.

"Ter, don't make me cum! Not yet! I want to fuck you, it's been too long!" he begged for me to slow down, to stop with the tease.

"I'm ready for you!" I told him. "Come and get it!" I stood up from kneeling and turned my naked body away from his. Bending over slightly, I felt him grab my ass hard from behind. With nowhere to brace myself, I prayed I could stay standing on my feet. Even the walls of the tent wouldn't hold me up. I heard him unwrap the condom package quickly, and it wasn't long before he thrust his hard cock deep into my pussy from behind. Jesus Christ, that felt amazing! I moaned as we both then fell to the floor of the tent.

As I lay next to the Scorpion on the cold tent floor, my head buried in his hairy chest, I closed my eyes to a time when life seemed simpler. Hearing him breathe quietly has he laid with one arm around me, fully passed out from the exhausting fuck we just encountered, I glanced over at my phone.

Messages from Sophia saying, "Where the fuck are you?!" drew me out of my comfort zone. I needed to head back to the beach and I needed to do that without waking my Scorpion.

As I slid his arm gently off of me, I grabbed my bikini and quickly threw it on. Seeing a towel in the corner of the tent, I picked it up and unzipped the tent flap and poked my head outside.

No one was around. The only sign anyone was there was the two empty beer bottles the Scorpion and I had left on the ground near the picnic table. I knew I was good to make my escape and disappear without my Scorpion knowing, glancing back as I did one last time to take all of him in. As I stood in the bar once again staring at my Scorpion and taking him all in as he leaned against the bar, everything in my body was telling me to go to him.

Sophia was shouting at me asking me, "Why the fuck are you still standing here, Ter?! Go to him! You know you regretted leaving him in the tent without even a goodbye!"

I stood there frozen, and then I caught his glance. He saw me. He moved forward to take a step. But as he did, I smiled at him, panicking as I waved and turned away. Sophia and Veronica followed.

"What the fuck Ter?! What are you doing?!" Sophia yelled.

I didn't answer. This night was all too much for me. I needed to get some air. My phone buzzed in my ass pocket as I walked faster away from the girls. Pulling it out to see who it was, I glanced down at the screen to a text from my Scorpion. I stopped. Paused. And then opened it.

"Where are you going?" it read. "You don't want to come say hi?" he asked.

I pondered my answer. Turning to Sophia and Veronica I said, "I just need a moment. You guys go get us a drink. I'm going to pop out for some air. I will be back."

They agreed.

As I slowly walked toward the door, I texted my Scorpion back, "Just getting air. I will be in soon."

He replied with, "If you don't, I will come find you," followed by a wink face emoji

This was the time I thought would have been a great time to not be a fucking nonsmoker! I needed something to take the edge off the nerves I was feeling, and I wished I had a cigarette to do just that!

Having the phone staring at me while in my hand, I thought to myself, *Fuck! I need to tell my Italian right now what I'm thinking.* I was so pissed off at his disappearing act that he needed to know this game of cat and mouse was no longer fun.

"Where the hell are you?!" I typed. And then I waited. Making my way through the crowed bar toward the front door. Staring down at the phone, I waited for it to light up.

"Seriously?" I wrote. "Did you fuck off on me?! Why did you even come tonight? Why play with me like that?!"

Silence.

My blood was boiling even more and so before stepping out the door, I made a quick stop at the shooter bar and threw back a shot. My phone buzzed in my hand.

"Not playing games," he wrote. "Why did

you leave the Cuban on the dancefloor?" he asked "I was enjoying seeing his hands all over your beautiful ass"

Unbelievable! I thought.

"I needed to get some air," I told him.

"You know I like to watch," he typed. "You make my cock throb," he said.

I smiled even through the anger

"Is your cock hard now?" I asked.

"What do you think?" he replied.

"Then come find me, damnit!" I yelled into the phone as I typed the words. "You know where I am!" I shut my phone off and threw it in my purse.

Pushing my way through the people to the front door, all I could think of was that I just needed to get out. I needed to breath some air and clear my head. Already feeling the effects of the booze, and the stress of the night, I decided I would just call an Uber and go home. It was clear my Italian wasn't coming for me. He once again disappeared.

Standing outside the club, I could hear the hum of the base inside. People came and went as I paced back and forth in the parking lot waiting on my ride. I had texted Sophia to let her know I was going home. She wasn't happy but I didn't care.

The fog was thick, and the air was cool. My mind busy with thoughts of the night. As I turned on my heel to check down the one side of the lot for the Uber, I heard an engine pull up behind me. Turning to see a black Lexus Rx beside me, I suddenly heard my heart pound outside my chest.

Even though the fog was heavy, I could see clear inside his car as the passenger door opened.

"Get in!" I heard him say.

I smiled as I slid my ass down on to the heated seat and closed the door behind me.

He revved the engine as he placed his hand on my knee. Pulling away from the bar, he turned and looked at me, "What took you so long?!"

Book Two Teaser

After The Bar Closes

My Italian knew exactly what he was doing when he made the reservations at his favourite restaurant. Known for his discretion, I heard him ask before he hung up the phone, "A table at the back in the private room for me and my date, please."

The waiter greeted us, led us through the charming yet sophisticated restaurant to the back to a private room that awaited us. There was a table set for two behind a red, plush velvet curtain that hung over the entry way. The lighting was low, and candles glowed atop the table. Music was playing, but it was so faint it was hard to make out the tune.

My Italian held my chair out for me and as I sat, I noticed the glance and the smile he exchanged with the waiter. He pushed my chair in gently and sat down next to me, taking my hand in

his. I still remember the feeling of thinking I could get used to this as his hand touched mine.

The waiter was handsome, and I knew this was by no mistake. My Italian knew beauty and enjoyed it when he saw it. I recall my Italian calling him Thomas as he thanked him for seeing us to our seats.

Thomas was tall – taller than my Italian – with dark, thick hair that had a slight curl to it. His look was more on an edgier side as he had the back of his head shaved, leaving more of the curl to the front with a sweeping strand over his forehead. His face was freshly shaven, exposing his strong jaw line and slight dimple cleverly placed in his chin. His shoulders were square, and I could see the peaks of his trap muscles under his crisp, white shirt. My eyes trailed down to his arms, where it was obvious that he was no stranger to the gym.

He smiled over at me as he asked my Italian if it was time to pour the wine.

My Italian gave a sly smile, indicating it was indeed time. He poured our glasses of wine and as he did, he came to stand beside me. I saw him glance down at me, moving his eyes towards the cleavage I was displaying from my loosely buttoned blouse. He smiled again, but this time at me. No one spoke as I felt my Italian place his hand on to my thigh and gently move its way under my skirt. Taking me a little by surprise, I jumped slightly. He spread open my thighs, making his

way to my vagina with his fingers. The waiter continued to stand there, smiling at me some more, as did my Italian.

I closed my eyes as I felt his fingers go deep inside me. He leaned into me and began to kiss the side of my neck as he brought his lips to my ear. It was then that I heard him whisper, "Undo his zipper baby."

While a little surprised, I didn't hesitate. I wanted to please my Italian. I knew this handsome waiter was handpicked just for me and for my Italian to enjoy. As I turned my head toward the waiter's crotch, I took my left hand and unzipped his pants. He had already turned his body to face me in anticipation.

My hand slid into the opening to grab a hold of his already hard cock, all the while feeling my Italian's fingers make love to me. With every touch he made, my body tensed, and I could feel my grip on the waiter's cock harden. His kisses filled my neck and his lips made their way back to my ear.

As I stroked the waiter, I heard my Italian say, "Suck it for me, baby. Please be my slut."

I turned away from my Italian and faced the waiter who stood before me with his cock in my hand. My mouth gently reached over his penis and I felt him shudder. He got harder as I made my way down his throbbing shaft with my mouth. My Italian moaned as he saw the pleasure on the waiter's face.

I continued to suck, hearing the waiter knock over some cutlery as he braced himself with the table. This went on for several moments as my Italian continued to fuck me with his hand. The feeling was intense and my desire to please my Italian grew stronger with every touch made inside me. His lips made their way to my ear once more, this time he thanked me by asking me to "...kiss me baby! Kiss me with his cum on your lips!"

My mouth continued to suck the waiter's cock until I could feel his body want to cum. The more excited the waiter got, the more excited my Italian got. And the more excited my Italian got, the more excited I became. I sucked the waiter's cock until he came in my mouth and with his warm, fresh cum, I made my way to my Italian. He opened his mouth for me to stick my cum-dripping lips onto his. He was stroking his penis as my tongue made its way around his mouth. His fingers were moving feverishly inside me and the intensity growing as he stroked himself harder and faster. He was breathing heavily now, and the two of us were cumming together, he in his own hand and me in his.

As our climaxes evolved and then came to an end, I opened my eyes to turn to look where the waiter had been standing not long before. He was no longer there. The red velvet curtain to the room had been drawn and only two poured, untouched glasses of wine on the table remained. My

Italian and I sat there for a moment trying to compose ourselves, his hand no longer inside me and now resting on my thigh.

Reaching across the table, he grabbed a crisp white napkin to clean himself up with. Wiping off his hand, he then grabbed one of the glasses of wine and passed it over to me. Grabbing the second glass, he held it up to the light to inspect it. He swirled the wine around the glass a moment, then after taking a sniff of it, he raised his glass and looked at me, smiling.

"Salute baby!" he whispered as he took a sip.

I live with my two amazing daughters, and I h...
that as I raise them, I continue to instill i...
that they are truly capable of doing any...
put their mind and their heart to! Ar...
my passion, my love for the writt...
played for all to see, I hope they se...
fact truth.

Kelson loves to socialize a...
Connect with her at the fo'...
https://www.facebook.c...
Instagram: @kelson_j_v...
Look for Kelson J on An...
bookshelf!
Visit her site at www.kelsonj.com a...
her newsletter to get updates sooner an...
exclusive promotional deals and future boo...
teasers!
If you enjoyed this book, please share your love by
leaving a review. It's how authors succeed in the
publishing world. Without the reader's love and
support, Authors would just be scratching words
on paper.
Thank you for your interest and your continued
support!

About The Author
Kelson J

Hi! I'm Kelson,

A little About Me

I was born in Toronto, Canada and grew up in
a small city nearby. As a child, I always knew I
wanted to be a writer. Stories bounced around in
my head and the characters became my friends
when I needed them to be. I dabble in short stories, poetry, and lyrics (but I have no musical abilities to speak of!), children's books, and now the
world of erotica! If my late grandma knew, I shudder to think what she'd say!
I've always travelled in my own lane and never felt
I needed to be anyone that I wasn't. Like Ter in
"A Russian & an Italian Walk into a Bar," I've never
apologized for being who I am.

Manufactured by Amazon.ca
Bolton, ON

12697362R00094

About The Author

Kelson J

Hi! I'm Kelson,

A little About Me

I was born in Toronto, Canada and grew up in a small city nearby. As a child, I always knew I wanted to be a writer. Stories bounced around in my head and the characters became my friends when I needed them to be. I dabble in short stories, poetry, and lyrics (but I have no musical abilities to speak of!), children's books, and now the world of erotica! If my late grandma knew, I shudder to think what she'd say!

I've always travelled in my own lane and never felt I needed to be anyone that I wasn't. Like Ter in "A Russian & an Italian Walk into a Bar," I've never apologized for being who I am.

I live with my two amazing daughters, and I hope that as I raise them, I continue to instill in them that they are truly capable of doing anything they put their mind and their heart to! And by seeing my passion, my love for the written word displayed for all to see, I hope they see that this is in fact truth.

Kelson loves to socialize and hear from her fans. Connect with her at the following links:
https://www.facebook.com/kelson.jwriter
Instagram: @kelson_j_writer_erotica
Look for Kelson J on Amazon, and add her to your bookshelf!
Visit her site at www.kelsonj.com and sign up for her newsletter to get updates sooner and receive exclusive promotional deals and future book teasers!
If you enjoyed this book, please share your love by leaving a review. It's how authors succeed in the publishing world. Without the reader's love and support, Authors would just be scratching words on paper.
Thank you for your interest and your continued support!

Manufactured by Amazon.ca
Bolton, ON